M000294092

THE HEAVENLY OAK

PHILIP BAUER

To my sponsor Ron Tewksbury

The Heavenly Oak Copyright © 2017 by Philip Bauer
Trifecta Publishing House
Vintage Hill Press - Imprint

All rights reserved. Except as permitted under the U.S. Copyright
Act of 1976, no part of this publication may be reproduced,
distributed, or transmitted in any form or by any means now known
or hereafter invented, or stored in a database or retrieval system,
without the prior written permission of the publisher, Trifecta
Publishing House.

This book is a work of fiction Names, characters, places, and incidents are the product of the author's imagination or are used ficti-
tiously. Any resemblance to actual persons, living or dead, business
establishments, events, or locales is coincidental.

Published in the United States of America First Printing: 2017
E- Book
ISBN -13: 978-1-943407-24-8

Print
ISBN -13: 978-1-943407-25-5

Trifecta Publishing House
1120 East 6th Street
Port Angeles, Washington
98362

TRIFECTA PUBLISHING HOUSE

VINTAGE HILL PRESS

Contact Information: Info@TrifectaPublishingHouse.com
Editors: Elizabeth Jewell, Diana Ballew
Cover Art by Rae Monet
Formatted by Monica Corwin

ONE

CHRISTOPHER

"I, even I, am he who blots out your transgressions, for my own sake, and remembers your sins no more." Isaiah 43:25

THE DRIVE HOME was like every other. I was preoccupied. The endless meetings and phone calls were hitting me in waves throughout the day. I was buoyed by the knowledge: It was Friday. I had two glorious days with no one asking anything of me.

The early spring rains were now a regular topic of conversation. The long hard winter had finally given up its grip. The drive-time announcer told a grateful audience the weather would be clearing up for the weekend. The windshield wipers were trying to keep up with the increasing downpour.

Reaching for the radio dial, I searched for an oldies station. I tried to remember the call letters and number of that new classic rock station I wanted to try.

Hearing the screeching of brakes, I immediately looked for the source of the ominous sound. Scanning left, I saw drenched, running pedestrians who tried to escape the deluge. Straight ahead was clear. The new radio station began blasting out its new format. The Joe Walsh guitar solo couldn't overcome the invasion of glass, crunching metal, and screams that came from a place deep within me.

I know now why people say that everything seems to be in slow motion. The braking sound I had heard came from a pickup truck hitting my car from the rear. As my head smashed through the windshield, I wondered why my airbags didn't work and if I would ever smell the sweet fragrance of freshly baked bread again. The sound of my mother's laughter, my first taste of ice cream, the games of kick the can, prom night, weddings, funerals; faster and faster the images flashed through my mind.

Sights and sounds that had been long forgotten were now vivid and alive. Random bits of information, both vital and ridiculous, flooded in. "Why didn't I ever tell her how I felt? The rain is going to wreck my suit. I loved the long walks I took with my dad before he died. That science project deserved an A, but Mr. Lange didn't like it. That's what I get for washing the car. I was leaning against the coffee table as everyone cheered my first step. Mom taught me how to draw. My newspaper is probably wet on the front porch. When I touched her hair for the first time, I knew that I had finally met 'the one'. Did I remember to call back that customer about his order? Is there life after death?" These were my competing thoughts as I saw the approaching pavement. Mind-numbing pain and the sound of shattering bone greeted my landing on that rainy Friday in late April.

Sticky moisture on my face gently woke me from a deep slumbering sleep. The shock of the last twenty seconds at the intersection of Pennington Avenue and 38th Street was slowly rising to the surface. It seemed as if it had happened long ago, to someone else, and yet it was still fresh in my mind.

Is this it? Twenty-three seconds stand between life and death? The sirens were quickly on the scene. Glass in my eyes prevented me from opening them. The pain was incomprehensible. People surrounded me, yelling and shouting orders. I knew they were trying to help. I was talking--yelling, really--and yet no one seemed to hear me.

"One, two, three," they yelled, as I felt myself being lifted. Blacking out is a term I had heard all my life, but it didn't seem to apply to my current state. I knew my brain wasn't allowing my body to feel the pain, but I didn't expect to be awake through all this. The sirens started up again, and this time they weren't as loud. The urgency and desperation I had first felt, to stay, to hang on, to go on, was now becoming increasingly irrelevant. The louder they yelled at me to "stay with us," the less I felt like I needed to.

Describing what came next as sleep is an understatement. I felt an overwhelming need to slumber, to curl up with a good book on a wintry day and doze off, that feeling you get when you want to drift into an afternoon nap after Thanksgiving dinner. They were desperately trying to keep me awake, but I was joyously retreating into a warm cocoon.

The moisture on my left cheek was not my blood; it was dew on the abundant clover that I saw when I opened my eyes. Now the sirens were replaced with the songs of birds singing in a tree somewhere close. Lying there, I felt a comforting, gentle breeze. My logical mind told me to be afraid, but that wisp of fresh air settled my nerves and took away all my brokenness.

The birds sang louder now with a chirping melody. I expected pain from what were broken ribs only seconds ago. No pain, but also no answers to the nature of my surroundings. Sitting in the clover, I felt warmth on my face. I got that spring-fever feeling I used to get as a kid when the first sunny day finally arrived. The hands that shielded my face from that awful landing now touched the deep green grass surrounding me. I found myself on the side of a hill, overlooking a deep valley. Looking out, it seemed I could see forever. The greens were vivid, and the flowers bright, with colors I had never seen.

The huge rolling basin was filled with an abundance of trees and large expanses of green and yellow pastures. A babbling brook sprang from a rock just a half mile or so down the hill. The water ran eagerly down the valley into a lake that shimmered with gladness at each new drop of its splashing friend. All the beauties around me appeared to understand each other: the brook and the lake, the birds and the wind, the warmth of the sky smiling down on the flourishing hillside. There was an overwhelming feeling that a newcomer was in their midst; it was a somewhat bewildered new neighbor sitting halfway up a magnificent precipice.

A childish notion came over me. It had been years since I had rolled down the side of a hill just because I felt like it. My grandmother had a hill behind her farmhouse that I used to love to roll down. The faster I rolled and the dizzier I became, the more I wanted to get up and do it again. Smiling broadly, and without hesitation, I lay down on my side and started to roll toward the meadow below. The softness of the green grass and the smell of the fresh air filled my spirit as I laughingly rolled down the hill. The meadow was approaching quickly as I giggled my way into its lap. I lay at the bottom, wondering if I should get up and do it again. My laughter echoed throughout the majestic crevasse before me.

The thought of sharing this event suddenly came to me. My Laura adores flowers and long walks. She would love this. My big brother, Johnny, would enjoy this, just like when we were kids behind grandma's house. Where were my family and friends? Did they know I was here? I expected to miss them, but instead, I felt a sense of peace that they would be along when they were supposed to be and that there was no hurry.

I thought it must be a dream, but I prayed I would never wake up. There was no logical explanation for what was happening, but I knew I didn't want to leave this place of peace.

I climbed back up the summit toward the place where I had first arrived. The higher I ascended, the more spectacular the view. It was as if I could see the whole world from here. Looking forward, I noticed a tree. A mighty oak sprawled its limbs across the very top of this mount. It was a rugged thing of beauty, beckoning me to bask in its shade at the top of the world.

TWO

✝

IT WAS obvious that this oak was no ordinary tree. The majesty of its huge trunk and leafy branches comforted me. Walking around the massive trunk, I felt the rough bark against my hands. Circling around the back of the tree, I looked out over another scene of breathtaking beauty. There was so much to take in that I almost missed what was right in front of me. A rope hung down from one of the tree's mighty arms, and on the end was an old tire. I remembered the tire swing at my childhood home. Simple things, like rolling down hills and tire swings ... how could I have forgotten those joys?

Grabbing the tire, I started to climb the tree. I was finding it difficult to climb with one hand while holding the tire with the other.

It was then that I heard a voice asking, "Do you need some help?"

Looking up into the tree, I saw a man holding out his hand and smiling. I was startled and yelped. Dropping the tire swing, I fell to the ground. A huge burst of laughter came from the man in the tree, shaking the branch he was sitting on. The fall didn't hurt; the clover had welcomed my landing. Propping myself up on my elbows, I strained to see the man in the tree. His laughter was contagious, and I soon found myself joining him. The swing made its way out to the end of its journey and was returning to the tree at a rapid pace.

"Look out!" said the voice.

I jumped up and turned just as the tire swing hit me in the chest and knocked me back down. Apparently, this was too much for the man in the tree. His merriment knocked him off the large branch and onto the ground. We were both snickering at my calamity, as the tire swung back and forth above our heads.

"You have got to watch out, that swing will get you every time," he said with a smile.

He stopped the swing, sat down, and leaned against the tree. I joined him, and we looked out over the valley in the shade of that mighty oak. We sat in silence, just listening to the birds singing their melody from the branches above our heads.

"You hear that song they are singing?" he asked, as he turned his head to look at me.

Gazing upward into the leafy canopy, I nodded.

"That's your song. They just came up with it today. Do you like it?"

Closing my eyes, I listened, as all the birds sang the beautiful refrain.

"I told them you would," he said, with a sense of pride you would only see from a loving father.

"Who are you?" I asked, looking into his friendly eyes. His face was familiar, and yet I was sure I had never seen it before. His dark wavy hair and the pleasant smile quietly assured me without his saying a word.

"I AM ... well, let's just leave it at that," he said.

"You are who?" I asked.

"No, not who, I," he said.

"I'm confused."

"I know, but it's okay," he said quietly.

"Am I dead? Is this the end?"

He stood and stretched. "It's only the beginning."

I stood next to him, and he put his arm around my shoulder.

"This is overwhelming. I have a million questions!" I said almost pleadingly.

"I knew you would; that's why I made this place for you. It was meant to put you at ease so we could have a chance to talk."

"Wait a minute, you made all this for me?" I asked.

He squeezed my shoulder and said, "Well, first of all, there are no minutes here, but yeah, I made this for you."

I asked again, "Am I dead?"

He stepped away, looked me up and down with a smirk, and said, "You look very much alive to me."

"Former things have passed away," he said over his shoulder as he started to walk down the back side of the hill, signaling me to follow. When I caught up to him, I saw that he had on hiking boots, faded jeans, and a white cotton shirt. I was surprised that I was no longer in my suit. I was now wearing my favorite jeans, hiking boots, and a new shirt that felt tailor-made.

"'Who shot JFK?' That's what you want to know," he said.

Surprised he could read my thoughts, I said, "It seemed important, until you said it out loud."

He was obviously amused. He looked at me and said, "Oh, Christopher, I am so glad you are here."

As we walked down through the grass and flowers, I looked up to see the source of the warmth on my neck and face. I noticed there was no sun, just a beautiful, bright blue sky.

We came to a dirt path that was cut in the grass.

"This way," he said.

We walked side by side, and the small rocks crunched under our feet.

"Where are we going?" I asked.

"We have some work to do," he said.

He gave me a playful jab in the ribs and took off running along the trail. I scampered after him, noticing that I wasn't getting winded. The harder I tried, the faster I ran, and the more energy I had. The path ran along a ridge and into a clump of trees between two hills. He disappeared around the bend. I struggled to keep up with him. The trail narrowed as I came around the bend. He was out in front running backwards and smiling.

"We are almost there!" he yelled.

He turned and ran quickly into the trees. The birds followed him, singing and chirping happily.

Running after him, I was reminded of the countless hours I played hide-and-seek as a child and how it never got old. That same youthful exuberance was with me now as I rustled through the low-hanging branches along the shady path. Suddenly, I came to a clearing in the woods. He was sitting on a log. In the middle of the expanse, surrounded by tall trees, sat a wooden barn.

"This is where we begin our work," he said, standing as I approached. He embraced me. "I am so excited for you to get started."

He opened the barn door, and the birds flew anxiously to their perches in the rafters of this ancient structure. The first thing I saw was a stable with a magnificent white horse in the stall. The animal whinnied and shook his mane as we approached.

"This is Regal," he said, gently stroking the white mane.

Regal blew air from his nostrils. This made him laugh. He promised the white beauty they would go riding soon.

The stall was clean and neat. A royal robe of purple and gold hung on the wall behind the horse. Next to it were two crowns; one of thorns, the other, a royal crown fit for a king.

"That robe and shiny crown look like they have never been worn," I said.

"They haven't ... yet," he said. "That other crown, I wore only once a long time ago. I keep it up there to remind me."

The large barn was cut in half by a floor-to-ceiling wall. The front section was the stable. We walked to the back of the stable toward an ornately hand-carved door.

Regal whinnied again as if to say, "Don't forget about your promise."

"I won't," he said over his shoulder as he closed the door behind us.

I stood in silence taking in the massive room. The floors were polished oak. On the right was a workbench that filled the full length of the wall. Woodworking and wood-sculpting tools and equipment lay neatly on the counter. In the middle of the room was a perfectly built round table with clay-sculpting equipment. Moist clay was laid out on a large white cloth. It appeared as though a project was about to start. Light shone through a large window on the back wall, letting in the beauty of the dense woods beyond.

On the left side of the room with his arms folded, he leaned against an elongated drafting table. The angled table was built all along the wall. There were several blueprints and plans spread open across the workspace. Additional stacks lay on shelves above the handmade desk. There was a beautiful golden compass, a long wooden ruler, and some freshly sharpened pencils placed neatly near the papers. On the back wall, under the window, sat two brown leather chairs and a coffee table. The sitting area was set off by the most intricately sewn, multicolored area rug I had ever seen.

He motioned toward the chairs. "Have a seat. This is my shop," he answered, before I could ask the question.

He sat in the chair on the right side of me. The chairs were slightly angled toward one another, and on the coffee table was a large, tattered book. I picked up the book. It was heavy and cumbersome.

"That is the story of your life. It's all in there. Would you like to take a look?" he asked, as he leaned back in the leather chair.

"I, I don't know for sure," I said, marveling at the name in gold on the spine of the book: Christopher Michael Lee.

"There is some really good stuff in there. Go ahead and see if I forgot anything," he joked.

I slammed it shut and abruptly stood. I paced the ornate rug beneath my feet.

"I know you still aren't sure what all this means, Chris, but it's going to be just fine, I promise," said my serene new friend.

"If that book is my life, then I died on Pennington Avenue today!" I cried. "And it also means I have to account for what's in that book, and I don't think I'm ready for that." I looked out the window to see a deer grazing on the tall grass.

He picked up the book and held it out. "Open the book to the last page. It should take away any doubt about its veracity."

I reached for the book and sat in the soft leather chair beside his. Running my hand across the red tattered cover, the realization started to set in. Reluctantly, I opened to the last page. There was a full account of my day. All the phone calls, the thoughts, the daydreams, triumphs, and frustrations of my last Friday on earth. At the bottom of the page was the last entry: "Left them en route to the hospital in an ambulance speeding down Pennington Avenue just past 43rd Street." Then a series of symbols I didn't recognize.

"What are those symbols?" I asked. "They look similar to the symbols you have on your plans and blueprints over there."

It didn't seem to bother him that I asked questions without waiting for the answers.

He smiled and said, "The symbols in both cases are mathematical. The symbols in your book are the mathematical equations that describe your physical body becoming a spiritual essence."

"So, it's my time of death?"

"It's the space on your line where your chemistry no longer was in need of physical structure and was transformed," he said.

"That's easy for you to say," I said, and the room filled with laughter.

Feeling a little more at ease, I slowly opened the book to the first page. There was a picture of me as an infant, lying in a blanket on the same round table that was still in this room in front of us.

"What's this?" I asked.

He pulled his chair closer and looked at the book with the pride of a proud father.

"That's your birthday!" he said excitedly. "I worked and worked on you until I got you just right, just ... Christopher."

I looked at him in bewilderment. I gazed at the large round table in the middle of the room. A chill went down my spine as I realized that on that table, in that clay, I was fearfully and wonderfully made. He touched the image on the page, and it took us to that moment. I found myself standing at the drafting table looking down at large blueprints and drawings. Looking back towards the table, I saw him putting the final touches on his clay masterpiece. The drawings and plans in front of me were both intricate and artistic. Mathematical symbols and equations beside beautiful drawings of me as an infant and at every stage of my development lay before me. Drawings of both my parents, with notes and equations, were on one of the larger pieces of parchment.

I watched in awe as he leaned down to gently blow his breath into the perfectly formed lips of the clay sculpture. The clay turned a lovely pink and began to squirm and coo. He leaned back looking at his creation and with a large grin said, "It is good!"

THREE

WHEN THE PAGE TURNED, I was back in the leather chair with my book of life in my lap. Struggling to take it all in, I laid the book on the table in front of us and stood. I gazed in silence, taking in the room. Slowly, I made my way past the potter's clay on the center table and toward the golden compass. The light from the window shone brightly on the shiny instrument. The plans that represented me were now long since put away. There, on his long drafting table, were plans for an upcoming project.

"This is where it all started?" I asked sheepishly.

"Not only for you, but for everything." He pointed at his angled desk. "That is where I laid the foundations of the earth."

"What are these?" I asked, as I looked at the plans on his table.

"Just something I am working on."

"You mean you are still making plans?" I asked.

"Always," He replied.

"If I've gotten this far, why do I still have work to do?" I strolled to the long carpentry bench on the other side of the room.

"Don't you want to continue to grow?" He asked.

"Well, I always liked the idea of eternal rest, with heavy emphasis on rest." I smiled.

"The universe was created to constantly expand and grow and you are part of that universe," He said.

Walking back toward the leather chair, I glanced out the window and saw the deer scampering into the woods. Sitting back down in the soft leather chair, I picked my book up.

"You said you would have to account for what's in the book. While that's true, don't you believe in forgiveness?" He asked.

"Well, yeah, but there is stuff in this book that I'm not too proud of."

He smiled and said, "I wasn't real proud of you at those times either, but are you sure those things are in the book?"

Gazing down at the book, I tried to remember one of the worst things I had ever done. I looked for that one thing I had never told anyone.

Finding the entry from that day I began to read. I knew I was getting close to the moment of my greatest shame. Scanning down the page I came to a blank space. The entries stopped. At the bottom of the page was an image of me. He leaned over and touched the image on the page. Suddenly, I was standing in the back of a dark and filthy alley watching myself curled up in the fetal position crying out in prayer. The prayer had just ended, and I watched as I stood up slowly and wiped the tears from my face. My younger self staggered out of that alley, quietly sobbing, "thank you." In the book, there was no mention of what the prayer entailed.

A sense of deep regret came over me. The many years I quietly carried that baggage had encumbered me in countless ways.

"There were things that happened to me and others as a result of that terrible night. Are they in the book?" I asked.

"Forgiveness does not mean there are no consequences," He explained.

"So, this is my judgment day?"

He leaned back in his chair and said, "I prefer the term 'Question and Answer Day'. There are always a lot of questions, and I love giving the answers," He said with a calming grin.

Returning to the book, we started at the beginning. Many entries at the beginning of my life fascinated me. Vivid details about my time in the womb, the day I took my first breath, and what my parents and doctors said. We spent a long time going from page to page, laughing and reminiscing about my early years. There were moments that brought me out of my chair, remembering such things as my first toy truck or a family vacation. It was so much fun to see those things in my childhood that I had forgotten. He watched with joy as I paced the floor with my book open. The simplest things seemed much more significant than the obvious celebrations of life.

Slowly, I sat and my smile faded as I came to the dreaded page. I read on as guilt and remorse consumed me. Memories flooded back to that early August day. I was seven years old, and we lived in the house on Trotter Way. The beautiful summer day begged a young boy to go swimming. Living next door was my best friend, Tommy Jacobs. Knocking on his back door, I was anticipating the fun of swimming in the pool at the empty house behind our backyards. The Martin family had moved out that prior spring and the real-estate agent insisted on keeping water in the pool. The six-foot-tall fence that surrounded the pool was in need of repair. Tommy and I had found a way into the pool area by way of a loose board next to the gate. It was a secret we kept from our parents and friends. We had the pool all to ourselves anytime we wanted to swim. When Tommy's back door opened, I remember being disappointed. Tommy had his little sister by his side. He explained that his mom had gone to the store and left him in charge of his sister, and that he would not be able to come out and play. This really made me mad, and I proceeded to try to change his mind. Pulling out all the stops, I decided to let our little secret out of the bag.

I leaned down to Elizabeth Joy and said, "Would you like to go swimming?"

She immediately started jumping up and down, screaming, and "Yes! Yes!"

Tommy was furious that I had broken the code of silence. Elizabeth Joy had already run back into the house to retrieve her favorite Barbie towel. After some continued badgering, Tommy and his four-year-old sister followed me to our secret swimming sanctuary behind the broken fence. We lifted the loose board and slipped through to the waiting pool. We instructed Elizabeth Joy to sit on the pool stairs where she could splash in the water. The sunny warmth beat down on three happy children, frolicking in the cool water.

The sudden sound of adult voices interrupted our fun. The real-estate agent had decided to show the home and was sliding the glass door aside to the pool area. We scampered out of the pool, grabbed Elizabeth Joy, and slid through the fence.

"I left my Barbie towel," said Tommy's little sister. We had her by each hand as we ran across the backyard.

"We can get it later," Tommy said.

Once we had escaped the wrath of the real-estate agent, we all giggled at our afternoon adventure. Drying off inside the screen porch, we recounted our narrow escape. Tommy and I turned to his blonde little sister and made her promise not to tell anyone.

After we were sure we had convinced her to keep the secret, we spent the afternoon laughing and telling the story over and over. We pondered the "what ifs" of getting caught and imitated the real-estate lady yelling at us. This brought another round of giggles from the three adventurers.

"What if that lady took my Barbie towel?" asked Elizabeth Joy.

"Nobody wants your old towel. We'll sneak over there tomorrow and get it," Tommy said. Elizabeth Joy stared across the backyard.

Mrs. Jacobs poked her head out on to the back porch to see three wet and happy children. She asked how we got wet, and Tommy immediately spoke up, explaining that we were playing in the sprinkler. This seemed to satisfy his mom. She said they had chores and that I should head home. We huddled once again, renewing our pact of silence. We promised the four-year old that we would get her towel back, and if she kept quiet, we would take her swimming again. Leaving the Jacobs' home, I was happy that we had had an adventure that lazy August afternoon.

The stroll back to my house is one that I have often pondered. The carefree moments before life-changing events are rarely recognized. This was the calm before grief's storm ... a deluge of human emotion that would wash away the joy and wonder of my youth. My hand shaking, I turned the page, remembering that awful day. He placed His hand on my arm and said, "This is some of the work I was talking about. You are doing very well."

"What does this have to do anything? That was so long ago, can't we just move on?" I pleaded.

Keeping His hand on my arm, He leaned forward and said, "To move forward, you have to quit expending energy in the wrong direction. Inertia in this realm will not allow backward motion."

Reassured, I looked down at the page and continued to read.

Sirens and doorbells woke me from my deep sleep. Police were at our door asking my parents questions. Looking down the staircase through the railing, I heard the name Elizabeth Joy Jacobs. Straining to hear them, I edged closer and heard they were looking for a lost girl and were doing a house-to-house search of the neighborhood. Hearing this, I gasped. The police officers and my parents turned their eyes toward me.

"Do you know this girl?" asked the taller of the two officers.

"Yes ... I ... she's my best friend's little sister."

The shorter officer walked toward the stairs, placing one foot on the bottom stair. He smiled. "Would you have any idea where she might be?"

"No!" I said a little too loudly.

My mother tilted her head, slowly walking up the stairs toward me. My father followed her up the stairs.

"Honey, is there something you know that could help these nice officers?" she asked sweetly.

"It's the Barbie towel!" I cried.

The police officers started up the stairs. I sat trembling on the top step.

My father bent down to look me in the eye. "What towel?"

"She left it at the pool, the Martin place. It's my fault!" I sobbed.

My mother turned to the officers. "That's across our backyard."

Both officers scrambled down the stairs, talking frantically into their walkie-talkies and running toward our backyard. We all followed the police. I watched more officers who had been waiting outside join in, running toward the pool. I met Tommy in the back-yard as we ran after our parents and police. We both stopped in our tracks when a gut-wrenching scream came from the depths of Mrs. Jacobs. We watched in horror as she fell to the ground at the sight of her baby girl being brought out from behind the fence. The stiff, life-less form lying in the officer's arms was wrapped in a Barbie towel.

Little Elizabeth Joy had drowned trying to retrieve her favorite towel. My knees buckled. The entire Jacobs family crumbled together on the grass screaming and crying.

If only I had listened to Tommy, if I wouldn't have pleaded with him to go swimming ... if ... if, I thought, as I ran to hide in my room.

The Jacobs sold their house and moved out of state within months of the drowning. I had tried to talk to Tommy, but it was never the same. The day the moving van drove away from their house, I stood crying in the street. Remorse and guilt consumed me for years. Eventually, I managed to put that night in a place hidden deep down inside, never to be opened again.

FOUR

I SLAMMED THE BOOK SHUT, lowered my head, and sobbed. A slight hand touched my face. Looking up, I saw the beautiful, smiling face of Elizabeth Joy Jacobs. She removed her favorite towel from her tiny shoulder and wiped the tears from my eyes.

"It's not your fault, Christopher," she said, in a sweet voice that seemed to transcend her years. "I was naughty that night. I snuck out my window and ran to get my towel."

She explained how she had slipped through the fence and saw the pool. It was a hot night, and she thought she should try the water. She went to the stairs and held onto the railing but the railing was loose, and she fell into the water.

"No one blames you for this. It was an accident," she said soothingly.

Years of pent-up guilt and remorse seemed to be purged from me in an instant. I was finally free.

"I get to go swimming with the Father anytime I want," she said joyfully.

This brought laughter from the three of us as we all embraced.

"Let's take a break and show Chris your favorite swimming hole," He said.

With that, Elizabeth Joy took me by the hand, and we instantly appeared on the banks of a serene pond. She ran out on a large log lying in the water. She turned and yelled ""Yippee!" as she jumped off the end of the log and into the crystal-clear water.

He smiled at me and said, "Go get her!"

I chased her off the log. He laughed and clapped His hands. He yelled to us that He was taking Regal for that ride He had promised and that He would catch up with me back at the shop.

"See you later, Abba!" she yelled.

He blew her a kiss and made His way up the grassy slope surrounding the small pond.

She turned to me, treading water, and said, "Tommy is gonna love this place."

"Is he coming soon?" I asked.

"Soon sounds like time, and there is no time," she said. "Tommy will be here when he is supposed to be, and we will all go swimming." She splashed me and swam away.

She showed me a trick the Father had shown her. We walked across the water. She stopped in the middle of the pond and dove into the water. Amazed, I dove in and chased her to the bottom.

She came up out of the water saying, "The Father wants you to meet Him back at the shop."

"Thanks, Elizabeth Joy," I said. We came out of the water.

She gave me a big hug on the bank, then ran up the slope, waving goodbye.

I instinctively knew where to go as I walked away from the pond. Glancing back at her swimming hole, I realized a great burden had been lifted from me. Turning toward the woods, I marveled that my clothes were completely dry. Walking down a shaded path, I knew there was much more work to do. Anticipation replaced fear as I headed back toward the Father.

The winding path through the woods opened to a huge meadow. Flowers and tall grass swayed in the light breeze. Butterflies danced across the large clearing. Suddenly, the birds began singing my song again, just as the Father rode His white horse into the meadow.

He raced back and forth through the tall grass, Regal proudly carrying his master. At the far end of the meadow, He turned and saw me. The beautiful white horse reared up and playfully shook his head. The majestic rider grabbed the horse's mane, leaning into his neck, and headed straight toward me at top speed. I heard Him laughing and egging Regal to go faster. I stood frozen in my tracks.

He approached, leaned down, grabbed me by the waist, and lifted me up onto His speeding horse. I grabbed His waist, and we sped down the shaded path. Leaves flew in our wake as we sped through the woods toward the barn. A mother bear and her cub tried to run alongside us as we dashed through the trees. The galloping hooves on the fertile ground awakened all living creatures as their creator whisked by.

The barn door swung open, welcoming us as we approached. Regal slowed to a trot as we went through the open door. Inside, we dismounted and He led his horse into the stall, petting his neck and whispering into his ear. Eagerly munching on his oats, Regal seemed satisfied that they had gone for a nice long ride.

Opening the door to the shop, I was welcomed by the aroma of a freshly cooked meal awaiting us on the low carved table in front of the leather chairs. The meal consisted of fresh salmon and bread. Tall glasses of cold spring water sat in front of each plate. We sat to eat, and He did something that surprised me. It was not exactly a prayer, but an acknowledgment of gratitude for the meal with His friend. The meal was created to give us a chance to simply relax and enjoy one another. We laughed about the look on my face in the meadow when He was bearing down on me.

"It was Regal's idea. I was just going along for the ride," He said.

I enjoyed the companionship while we ate our meal of fish and bread. What a contrast to the countless hours I spent with family, eating dinners in front of the television.

We finished our meal and leaned back in our chairs. The plates and glasses disappeared from the table.

"Loaves and fishes are always good," I joked. "Is that the same meal You fed the five thousand?" I asked.

He smiled. "Fifteen thousand, four hundred and seventy-three men, women, and children. The twelve were frantically trying to figure out what to do with all those folks."

He explained how they all settled down, both the crowd and the twelve, once they were fed. It was amazing to listen to this first-hand account of such a famous historical event.

He looked at the book on the table.

"Well, are you ready to continue?" He asked.

I nodded and picked up my book. The entries continued to amaze me. The smallest details about people, places, and situations were written in my book of life. But blank spaces continued to appear on pages, too.

I looked up and asked, "I know you took these things out, but do you remember what they were?"

"Once you told me about it, there was no longer anything to remember. You carried around a lot of junk," He said.

The entries were also filled with all the good things I had done. I always thought the book of life would be filled with only my wrong-doings. I was finding that He delighted in writing at length about my triumphs. The smallest kindnesses were written down. He sat quietly in His chair watching me read the story of my life from His perspective. The perceptions I had about myself and how others saw me were seen through a cloak of regret, pain, fear, and doubt. As I continued to read, I realized all the missed opportunities and dreams I had laid aside because of my vision of who I thought I was.

Turning the page, I saw an image of a notebook. Staring at it, I began to remember where I had seen it before. It was the school notebook I had carried with me in junior high school. It was the notebook that no one knew about. These pages were filled with the beginnings of many short stories and poems. When I was supposed to be studying, I would open that spiral bound book of dreams and escape into my imagination. Listening to the voices of others would compel me to stop before ever finishing. My parents thought I was a dreamer who was never going to pass my classes. They knew I had an interest in writing, but always told me it was a waste of time. The constant "drum of doubt" finally drowned out the passion I had for writing. Walking home from school, I remember pulling the tattered blue notebook from my backpack and tossing it into a dumpster behind Crane's Pharmacy. As the crisp fall leaves were trampled beneath my feet on my way home, so were my dreams of becoming a writer.

A rustling of paper brought my attention back to Him. He smiled and slowly turned the pages of my long-forgotten notebook.

"There is some great stuff in here," He said.

He handed me my old blue notebook. I was amazed to see my handwritten thoughts and poems from so long ago. I noticed that all of them were finished. There on the table were stories and poems written in my handwriting through high school and into college. There were several magazines also lying among my writings. Leaning forward, He picked them off the table and handed them to me. Bewildered, I opened them to short stories and poems that would have been written by me and then published in these magazines.

My path had been made for me, but I had had little faith in myself and listened to those around me instead of that quiet voice, deep down inside my soul.

"You were never meant to work at that job you loathed," He said soothingly.

He explained how my writing would have never made me rich but would have given me much joy. He told me that I was supposed to become a teacher who would eventually volunteer to teach adults how to read and write. The classes would have been held at the antique bookstore that I often browsed on Saturday mornings. The same bookstore would have become available to buy through a long-standing friendship with the owner. He would have allowed me to pay him off over several years, and I would have owned my favorite bookstore. I sat wide-eyed, astonished at the life I could have led. *So, that's why I was so drawn to "The Turning Page" bookstore,* I thought. The owner, Jacob Rinehart, had become a friend of mine. We spent hours talking about books and authors over freshly brewed coffee in the front of his store. Each time the front door opened, a tiny bell would welcome another customer into this quaint world of old books and hardwood floors. Jacob would tell me about wanting to retire, but he did not want the store to close. He would ask me about buying his place, but I never dreamed it was possible. It was one of those dreams that were fun to entertain on a Saturday. But the dawn of another Monday morning would always crush the delusion.

Regret settled over me as I thought of the hope that sat before me for so many years. It was obvious now that this had always been my path. Fear of failure and self-doubt kept me from listening.

"No regrets, Chris," He said.

"But there was so much wasted time," I replied.

"It was a moment's sunlight fading in the grass," He said.

I looked up from the book.

He leaned in and softly asked, "Did you think that was your only chance to attain your dreams?"

"Well, I always thought that we had a life, and then we come up here to rest and praise you."

"The best praise is a dream that is realized. That is the most beautiful accolade I can imagine," He explained. He leaned forward in His chair. "It's true that there is rest here. Rest from pain, fear, anguish, and the missing of the mark. That does not mean there is no work. We just do what we were meant to do instead of what we had to do."

He pointed at plans on His drafting table.

"I am still making plans because it's what I love to do. I created you in my likeness, which means I want you to continue to make plans and work on your dreams. The only people here with harps are those who wanted to learn to play them or build them," He said.

I smiled and asked, "Where is the cloud I have been assigned?"

His thundering laughter shook the giant window behind our heads. The feeling of complete belonging overwhelmed me as I sat with my new friend and constant companion.

FIVE

THINKING of all the time He was spending with me made me wonder if there were others that were now wanting and needing His attention. Sensing my thoughts, He reminded me there was no time here, that He wanted to enjoy this space with me, and that we could and would do much more of this.

He stood and clapped his hands. "Let's go to the city."

I slowly rose from my chair, placing my book of life on the table. "The city?" I asked.

"Yes, there is something I have prepared for you." He placed his arm around me and we walked past His beautiful white horse and out of the ancient barn. As we walked through the forest, He pointed left and right and up into the trees explaining how He created all the beauty that lay before me.

He said hello to birds calling each by name as we passed.

"Say hello to Christopher," He said.

The thick forest chimed in unison.

We came through the trees, and I recognized the path along the ridge where I had first followed Him. On the hill to my right stood the mighty oak with the tire swing swaying slightly against a light breeze. The bright blue sky cast a perfect backdrop on the endless rolling hills and valleys. He turned left down the hill. Looking toward the horizon I saw a gleaming skyline of an ancient city.

We reached the bottom of the hill. We walked side by side down a wide dirt, tree-lined road toward the city.

"Are you ready to continue?" He asked.

"I left my book back at the shop," I said.

"I think I can remember what is written down," He said, smiling. "Do you want to talk about your dad?" I stopped in my tracks and started to kick the dirt and small rocks in the road. Looking down, I reluctantly agreed. He reminded me of the many things that I did growing up that were contrary to my father's rules. I was taken back to those days in my childhood home. The smells, sights, and sounds of youth came flooding back. Situations that I had tucked away long ago were being brought to light as we walked the road toward the city.

My father had been strict. That was the official term we used. The church we attended as I was growing up took the passage in the Bible, "spare the rod and spoil the child," quite literally. It was so much a part of their culture that they actually had a fundraiser once in which they sold wooden paddles. A member of the congregation had a woodworking shop. He brought his creations to services, displaying them on a table at the back of the church. My father bought the largest one he could find and proudly showed others his new purchase. This long wooden paddle became a symbol of fear and shame as punishment was given out in the basement of our family home.

To say he spanked me would suggest a few light swats on my backside. The reality was I was beaten and left whimpering and soaked in my own urine on the basement floor. Through sobbing gasps, I was made to thank him for the "correction" I received. This ritual continued through my childhood and into my early teens. The dissent started small, but as I grew, so did my rebellion toward my father, his church, and his rules. Drinking his wine and beer began in my early teens. I would add water to his big jug to keep the level up.

He kept a case of beer on the landing going into the basement. Under the guise of using the basement bathroom, I would take two beers as I headed down the stairs. The bottle opener was hidden in the ceiling. Gulping down beer during the commercials of our favorite television show became my ritual. The frequency and amount rose quickly through my teen years. The need for more oblivion pushed my dependency over the line from 'problem drinker' to alcoholic.

The relationship I had with my father was complicated. I wanted his approval, all while doing everything I could to break his rules. I was in church every week, participating in the youth program and choir. My parents were longtime members of this church and had gained respect from the congregation. Drinking was now a daily occurrence, and my ability to hide it was becoming increasingly difficult. The collision of my dual lives had finally come to pass when, in a drunken stupor I danced on the tables of a potluck dinner, and proceeded to throw up on the Pastors wife. This son of a deacon and deaconess was asked to leave the congregation.

The shame I brought on my parents for my actions was my sick way of getting them back for the way I was raised. Rumors and innuendo ran rampant through the church, and they were left to explain why their son was no longer attending. My Pastor and my parents thought I should seek some outside help from a counselor.

The counseling sessions brought out my long-hidden anger and shame. To my father's great credit, when he was asked to join me with my counselor to talk about our relationship, he showed up ready to address any and all issues. That day was a pivotal point in my life. My father took responsibility for his part, and I took responsibility for mine. We walked out of that session truly close for the first time in our lives.

It was strange to talk about all this and not feel that pain in the pit of my stomach. The ability for Him to just listen to me, as we walked toward the city, was so refreshing. He obviously knew all of this, but did not feel the need to interject.

"I'm glad you let me just talk," I said.

"Your relationship with your dad ended up being a good one," He said.

I thought about the last years of his life and all the good times. The days before the dementia began to take him away. I smiled at the thought of playing card games and checkers with him. I used to relish the long walks to the river near our family home.

The last time I had seen my father was Thanksgiving weekend five years ago. The dementia had become so bad that my mother could no longer take care of him at home. He was living in a rest home several miles from their house. I took a trip home to have our last Thanksgiving together as a family. My father had withered since I had seen him last. He was in a wheelchair near the nurses' station when I exited the elevator. He was having a lucid day and immediately recognized me. We had a quiet lunch together in the cafeteria. I have always cherished that time we had together.

Profound sadness rushed over me, realizing that my mother was now facing the loss of her youngest son while still grieving the loss of her husband of sixty years.

"She will be here when she is supposed to be," He said, touching my shoulder. "There is someone who has been waiting for you."

He pointed down the tree-lined road toward the city. I turned my head and saw my father standing in the middle of the road. He saw me and started to laugh. I ran toward him yelling with glee. We hugged in the middle of the road. The bitterness dissolved in our embrace. All that remained between us was love.

"Peter, open the gates, Christopher is here!" the Father proclaimed.

My dad leaned over and whispered in my ear, "You are going to love this."

I realized that while we were walking, we had traveled a great distance and were now standing outside a massive wall in front of two grand gates. I heard the whinny of a horse behind me just as a trumpet sounded beyond the walls. I turned to see Regal, His beautiful white steed.

He was holding the reins. "Hop on, Christopher."

I petted Regal's nose and heard a great crowd cheer inside the gates. A purple blanket lay across the horse's back with my name embroidered along the bottom. He helped me up on the horse and started to lead the mount toward the gates. My dad walked alongside, gleaming with pride. A tall, rugged man opened the giant gates as we approached. Looking down, I saw the man waving and yelling, "Welcome!" over the cheering crowd.

"Thank you, Peter!" He said.

He led us through the thick walls of the city. As we cleared the entrance, another trumpet sounded and a mighty roar went up throughout the expansive courtyard. There were millions of people awaiting my arrival. They were clapping and cheering as He led us through the crowd. The citizens of heaven rushed through the golden streets to greet us. We made our way through the welcoming parade into a large city park. A gazebo sat in the center with a "Welcome Home" banner hanging from it. There were picnic tables lined up for miles filled with food and drink. He led me through the park past the tables and toward the gazebo. Music filled the air as we approached. He tied the reins to the stairs of the white, wooden gazebo as I dismounted. I followed alongside Him up the steps. He put his arm around me and raised His other hand. The entire throng quieted instantly.

"This is Christopher, my good and faithful son. Please welcome him into paradise!"

SIX

A THUNDEROUS EXPLOSION of joy rose up from the millions standing before me. My dad stood at the foot of the stairs cheering and patting Regal as the crowd continued to celebrate.

Tears of joy streamed down my face as He hugged me.

"It is appropriate that we celebrate and be glad, for Christopher was dead and is alive again; he was lost, but now is found," He proclaimed.

He led me to the table inside the gazebo and waited for me to sit in the chair. The crowd quieted when He turned to the masses.

"Let's eat!" He said.

He gestured to my dad to be seated. He then served us the most wonderful meal I had ever seen. We shared the feast, laughed, talked, and sang songs. The celebratory atmosphere was intoxicating and seemed to last forever. When we were finished, He asked politely if some people could help clean up. He rose from the table and told Regal to head back to the barn. His horse snorted, clearly not wanting to miss out on all the action.

"Come on, guys, I have something to show you," He said.

He winked at my dad, who seemed to know something I did not.

We walked down the stairs of the gazebo and toward the many rows of tables. People I had never met were telling me that they were glad I was there and welcomed me home. We walked for miles through the city park, greeting and acknowledging those around us. As we wound our way through the green grass, it struck me that people here were busy. It felt as though they had stopped whatever they had been doing to celebrate my arrival. People were going from place to place as if it were a workday. The only difference was they seemed genuinely happy about it. I watched as shop owners reopened their stores with customers milling about. Theaters and architecturally perfect office buildings were bustling with activity.

Sensing my confusion, He explained.

"They all have a purpose and want to do what they had only dreamed of on earth. I have given each a gift and a passion. We do not just sit around on clouds for eternity. We are always striving for new and satisfying challenges that enhance our gifts and ignite the passion."

I was astonished by the sense of perfect order. Everyone was doing exactly what they were meant to do.

At the edge of the city park was a street paved in gold, with a tree-lined boulevard running down the center. There were no cars, but everyone seemed to arrive at their destinations as quickly as they were supposed to. We crossed the street and stepped onto a curb made of a translucent green and red stone. It reflected light as we passed.

"We are almost there," He said, quickening his step. "We have been preparing a place for you."

We hurried down a golden street lined with shops and businesses and rounded a corner. He stopped and stepped to one side. I slowly proceeded past him, down the sidewalk. There, in front of me on the corner, was a bookstore. And this was not just any bookstore; as the sign indicated, it was 'Christopher's Books.' A grand opening banner hung in the window. The look and feel of the building was perfectly suited to my taste. It was nineteenth-century architecture with shutters and large paned windows. As we entered, the smell of freshly brewed coffee and old books filled my senses. Shelves of books from floor to ceiling lined two walls and lower shelves throughout the middle of the large store. In front were couches and chairs, and to the left a coffee bar. Light streamed through the front windows, creating a warm and welcoming atmosphere.

He and my dad sat in the chairs as I ran around the store whooping and hollering. Toward the rear of the store was a spiral staircase leading to the second floor. I climbed the stairs to an immaculately appointed living space. The large loft with hardwood floors was furnished with my favorite furniture and artwork. Exposed brick walls and track lighting were exactly what I had always wanted. A golden retriever puppy was lying on an area rug in the middle of the floor.

I knew his name instinctively and called, "Come here, Shakespeare!"

He wiggled his way over to my leg and lay on his back for a scratch.

After searching every room of my brand-new home, I bolted down the spiral stairs with Shakespeare on my heels.

"This is perfect," I said.

He smiled and my dad clapped his hands with joy. He stood and moved to the center of the store. He pointed at the display on the round table. A sign read, "Special reading from owner and author, Christopher, this Saturday."

"You can read one of those stories that you would have written and would have published, had you followed your dreams, or you can write a whole new story," He said.

I beamed. All my dreams were coming true.

"Before you do that, let me show you one more thing," He said.

He walked out of the shop and down the street. We followed and came to a large pillared structure that appeared to stretch into infinity. Steps led up to ornate doors lining the front of the massive building. Carved in granite next to the middle doors were the words, "Library of the Ages."

"The store was your dream, and it will fill you with great satisfaction for as long as it is supposed to. Remember, we are always looking to grow and learn. This building houses all the knowledge of the universe written in books," He explained.

I stood in awe in front of the carved granite. I reached out and traced the letters with my fingers. People were constantly going in and out of the thousands of huge golden doors to the right and left of us. We walked toward the doors and they graciously swung open. My dad and Shakespeare followed us into the foyer of the library. Looking straight up, the pillars led toward an ornate ceiling I could barely see. To the left and right were shelves and shelves of beautiful books. Polished granite floors reflected the light coming through the floor-to-ceiling windows, washing the foyer in a golden hue. The main floor was filled with millions of tables where I could see thousands of people quietly reading and milling about.

"Why do people still read to get access to information?" I asked.

"You are wondering why we do not have computers?" He asked.

My dad laughed.

"First of all, reading is a calming and enjoyable activity that cannot be replaced. Having said that, the speed at which you can now assimilate knowledge is far beyond your former understanding," He explained.

We started toward the grand staircase that led to the many floors and balconies that lined the great library. I picked up my new puppy as we ascended the stairs. We went up and up until we reached what I had counted as the 800th floor. I leaned over the marble railing looking down into the giant chasm of golden light and balconies lined with beautifully bound books.

He stopped when he noticed my awestruck expression.

"By the way, because the universe continues to expand, so does the knowledge. That means this structure is constantly expanding to accommodate the breadth of that new information."

He turned and walked down an aisle between two of the many tall shelves covering that floor. We followed Him until He reached an empty space on one of the many shelves. He slid a red tattered book into the empty space. I recognized that it was my book of life.

"I checked this one out recently and wanted to return it," He said.

"Is this why we came to the library?" I asked.

He put His arm around me as Shakespeare wriggled through my legs.

My dad followed as we walked to the railing.

"I keep telling you that we are constantly striving to grow, right?"

"Yes," I stammered.

"There will come a moment when the master librarian will need a bigger challenge and she will need to move on. When that happens, this will become your responsibility. You will be the master librarian for the Library of the Ages."

My knees buckled a little. He held me up. My dad came up beside me and patted me on the back, grinning from ear to ear. Shakespeare sensed something good was happening and joined in the celebration by wagging his tail. I began to weep tears of great joy at the opportunities that had been laid before me.

"Thank you for always believing in me, even when I could not believe in myself," I whispered, as I held Him close in a grateful embrace.

He held me tight.

"Your happiness is the sweetest prayer."

We continued to tour the Library of the Ages, reading concepts and ideas that I would never have been able to imagine. The sheer fun of learning new things and delving into the history of the universe captivated me. I ran from floor to floor and room to room. The little golden puppy slid and slipped his way trying to catch up as He and dad followed, smiling with pride.

When we exited the front doors, I was completely overwhelmed. I stood on the front steps overlooking the golden city. I felt the need to sit and drink in the moment. Lowering myself onto the top step, I leaned against one of the mighty pillars and closed my eyes. I felt Him sitting next to me. I opened my eyes. We were once again under the mighty oak on top of the hill.

Startled, I looked around, confused, but was reassured when He patted my shoulder.

"I thought you might need to take a breath," He said.

"Where are Dad and Shakespeare?"

"He took the puppy back to your store."

The anticipation of a future filled with purpose and direction sparked my imagination. I excitedly told Him of my plans for the store and the books I wanted to write. Listening intently, he gazed over the vast valley before us. He knew so much more than He was telling me, but patiently listened to every last dream I had. When He sensed I was done, He slowly stood.

Following His lead, I stood beside Him.

"I was just sitting here thinking how glad I am that I made you, Christopher. You are truly a joy to behold."

"Are you leaving?" I asked.

He put His strong arm around me.

"I will never leave you or forsake you, but I do have many things to do and plans to make. If you ever need to just talk or need help with anything, I will meet you right here under this tree," He said.

With that, He descended the hill. I stood by myself, but never again alone, under the mighty oak tree with the tire swing swaying gently in the breeze.

SEVEN

THE PREACHER

"Beware of false prophets, which come to you in sheep's clothing, but inwardly they are ravening wolves." Matthew 7:15

THE MUSIC SOARED ON STAGE. The lights came up when the announcer started his scripted introduction. A garishly lighted cross stood twenty feet high on the television stage. A lone figure stood backstage awaiting his nightly cue. His hair was perfectly coiffed and his Armani suit tailored to his middle-aged frame. Stress had been the order of the day. He had just met with his financial council of elders and had been informed that income was down for the third month in a row. The ministry of Apostle Jeremy Addison Hart was running out of money.

The elders suggested that the Apostle might need to sell at least one of the homes that the church had supplied him. They also thought it was no longer fiscally responsible to have two private jets on the books. He vigorously argued that God's apostle needed the planes and multiple homes to show the world that God was blessing his ministry. The pressure to downsize and the need to raise more money were raining down on the televangelist. The adversity was giving him ulcers and constant headaches.

Knowing the show must go on, he hit the stage with his usual charisma and sparkling smile. The studio audience roared. The television cameras greeted his arrival on the stage; he was bathed in colored lights. The vision that splashed on the large screens was one of a handsome middle-aged man with silver and black hair and a smiling tanned face. His golden hue came from stage makeup used to cover his increasingly pale visage. He strutted across the purple carpet toward the front of the stage.

The music died down and the applause waned. Jeremy Addison Hart stepped into the spotlight to deliver his message. The camera zoomed in for a close-up just as he raised the Bible in his left hand. His smile faded as he attempted to voice his introductory remarks. Pain began running down his arm, and his headache was now overwhelming. The Bible fell from his Rolex-clad hand. He clutched his chest, and his audience started screaming. An instant metamorphosis from perfection to hideous anguish washed over his face. Mayhem broke out. The television staff and employees of Hart of God ministries scrambled toward the stage. The persuasive preacher that had created the largest television ministry in the world lay crumpled in the spotlight he had craved his entire life.

The pain in his head and down his left arm was gone. He opened his eyes. Soft, green clover and the canopy of a large oak tree had replaced the colored stage lights and purple carpet. He sat up slowly, wondering what had just happened. The sermon he was about to deliver was still running in his head, but the financial stress of his empire was no longer weighing him down. He leaned against the trunk of the old oak tree. Looking around, he saw a clover-filled meadow in front of him, surrounded by tall trees, and the lyrical sound of a piano played in the distance.

The tune sounded familiar. It was a hymn he had learned growing up in church. Bracing himself against the tree, he stood to find the source of the music. Walking slowly around the trunk of the oak tree, he noticed a dilapidated country church nestled amid the trees at the back of the meadow. A gravel road ran past the white sanctuary and into the forest. A bell started to clang in the rickety steeple tower. Jeremy instinctively looked down at his watch. The diamond-encrusted timepiece was gone. It was then that he noticed he was wearing a T-shirt, faded jeans, and work boots.

Someone drugged me, stole my watch and clothes, and left me out here in the middle of nowhere, he thought.

"The whole world will be looking for me," he grumbled.

He strutted toward the sound of the piano. As he approached the front of the white church, he noticed some of the windows were missing and it was in bad need of a paint job. Taking his first step up the stairs, he didn't notice the wood had rotted and his foot went straight through. This small calamity led to a full-blown tantrum as he busted against the front door.

The door flew open hitting the wall with an echoing crash. Jeremy took in the room. Light streamed in through the windows on both sides, revealing many missing pews. Dust and old leaves covered the floor. There was a stage in front with a pulpit on the right side. On the left, a man sat at an old upright piano playing "Farther Along" with one finger.

"Hey! I have been robbed. Have you got a phone?" Jeremy shouted.

The man at the piano stopped playing. Jeremy noticed that he appeared to be in his early thirties, and that he had dark hair and a short-cropped beard. He wore a denim work shirt, jeans, and the same kind of work boots Jeremy was now wearing.

"Why are you shouting?" asked the man at the piano.

"Something has happened. I was drugged, robbed, and left out here in the boondocks!" Jeremy said.

The young man looked at him and smiled broadly.

"It will be okay, Jeremy. I promise."

Jeremy took a step back.

"How do you know my name?" Are you responsible for this? Did you kidnap me for money?"

Uproarious laughter poured out of the man as he stood and walked to edge of the stage. He sat on the center steps still chuckling and shaking his head.

"What is so funny?" Jeremy asked.

"I am the one responsible for your being here. It's really great to see you," he said.

Jeremy walked slowly toward the front of the chancel. He cautiously lowered himself into the front pew.

"You are safe, no one will hurt you," the man said in a calming voice.

His words calmed Jeremy's anxiety instantly.

"Sorry I had to interrupt your sermon, Jeremy. I guess I just couldn't let you spew that garbage as your followers go without. That's not my idea of what a shepherd should do."

Jeremy bristled. No one had ever confronted him about his ministry. "My followers know I am always looking out for their best interests. My insights and revelations of scripture have transformed the lives of millions! My flock give freely to my ministry so that we can usher in the kingdom."

The man shook his head.

"Your *insights*? First of all, a lot of the revelations you supposedly came up with were just regurgitated theories others had. You thought no one would research them, so you stole ideas from others and called them revelations from God. It worked to your advantage and your empire grew. But the money and power seduced you, and you forgot the real reason for ministry."

The man seemed to intimately know his life and his business. The televangelist wondered if his offices had been bugged or if there had been an investigator hired to research his background. Instinctively, Jeremy knew that he could not hide from this man.

"I have people who are going to be looking for me, whoever you are. You will be in a world of hurt. Kidnapping the apostle of the Hart of God ministries is not a good idea, young man!"

The bearded man chuckled and shook his head. He rose and joined Jeremy in the front pew. Eyes filled with love and compassion stared back at Jeremy. "You were not kidnapped, but a ransom has been paid for you."

Jeremy sprang to his feet. "I'm out of here!" He bolted for the open door at the back of the church. He looked over his shoulder and shouted, "Do not try to stop me!"

As he marched through the leaves and side-stepped broken pews, he tripped over a stack of hymnals lying on the dirty floor. He fell and the books toppled around him. Jeremy noticed one of the books was different from the rest. It was larger and red. Strangely drawn to it, he picked up the tattered volume. Gold letters on the spine read: Jeremy Addison Hart.

He slowly stood and started back toward the front of the small sanctuary. The young man in the front pew was looking back at him smiling.

Jeremy waved the book in the air. "What is this?"

"It's your book of life," the man answered from the front pew.

"Yeah, right," Jeremy smirked.

"Go to the last page."

Jeremy looked at him incredulously but followed his instructions. Opening to the last page, he read: "Jeremy Addison Hart left them from the stage of the television studio." This was followed by a series of unrecognizable symbols that looked mathematical.

"Is this a joke?" Jeremy asked.

The man stood, turned, and answered. "You had just come out of that meeting about finances. As you adjusted your tie in the back-stage mirror you were wondering if you could deliver another sermon that would inspire your audience to give. You were exhausted, your stomach and head were aching, and your left arm began to hurt. By the time you walked through the curtain, you knew there was some-thing wrong. You noticed the attractive blonde in the third row on the right side and the voluptuous redhead in the center section in the fourth row. Your lustful thoughts quickly subsided when the pain in your left arm increased. As you raised your hand to use the Bible as a prop, the pain became unbearable. There came a moment, right before everything went black, that you realized this could be the end. It was a fleeting and horrifying thought as you crumpled on the carpet. When you woke up under that oak tree out there, you thought you had been kidnapped. Is that how you remember it?"

Jeremy stood with his mouth open, listening to the man talk in intimate detail about those terrifying moments. No one ever knew about his nightly ritual regarding the attractive women in his audiences. The full description of his physical pain and inner thoughts was disturbing. The realization of what he was being told began to enter his conscious mind. He returned to the front pew, placed the book beside him, and put his head in his hands. His mind began to race.

"Am I dead?" "Did I have a heart attack?" The answers to those and other questions came to him without a word being spoken. This man was answering his thoughts.

"Who are you?" Jeremy finally asked as he looked up into the man's eyes.

The young man tilted his head slightly and said, "You have professed to know me for years. You have lined your pockets using my name. So, who do you say I am?"

EIGHT

THAT LAST PHRASE resonated with Jeremy. He had heard and preached about that phrase many times. To be asking the same question as Pilate, and receiving the same answer, reduced Jeremy to a quivering mass. He slid off the pew and fell on shaking knees.

Two strong hands reached down and grabbed his shoulders. Jeremy was lifted to his feet.

"Welcome home, Jeremy. We have a lot of work to do,"

"This is not what I expected when I got to heaven," Jeremy said.

"I'm sure," came the reply.

He handed Jeremy the red tattered book, and they sat on the edge of the stage. Jeremy was very fearful to look inside the book. Still, he opened it and started to read. Every detail about the plans to make Jeremy Addison Hart were there. He was shown the potter's clay where he was created. Reading the early details of his life brought back many memories.

Jeremy was the only child born to Harold and Lorna Hart. His father was a struggling advertising man, whose efforts brought in little money - only promises for future riches. Jeremy's mother Lorna was a stay-at-home mom. A religious woman, Lorna read the scriptures daily. Talking to her husband, she eventually convinced him that there was more to the scriptures than was being preached in the churches. Harold listened with the ear of an advertising man. He saw an opening in the marketplace, a niche. The more Lorna spoke to him about what she called the "prosperity gospel," the more he was convinced she was on to something. She contended that the Bible clearly states that God wants us to be rich. She had many scriptures that when taken out of context seemed to suggest that very thing. She was telling Harold this to inspire him, but he heard what he wanted to hear. Harold knew that in marketing if you had a new twist on an old idea, you could be successful.

Harold decided to get a license to preach. He took a correspondence course from a mail-order seminary called Preach the Word Ministries. The course took six months to complete and cost him a grand total of $850. This little fact was later hidden as he grew to be a prominent radio and television evangelist. As the ministry grew, so did young Jeremy. Born into a life of watching his father work a crowd and manipulate the scripture for financial gain made Jeremy cynical. One summer in his late teens, he rebelled against his father by joining another church. He attended their summer Bible camp. He met people who actually lived the life they professed.

After high school, Jeremy decided the best way to become his own man was to join the navy. He traveled the world, but the lures were too much for a sheltered preacher's son, and he nearly drowned in his own excesses. By the end of his four-year naval career, he had experienced many of the "lusts of the flesh" he had heard about growing up. His father was in poor health but still running the church and a Bible college. Jeremy had gotten a girl "in trouble" and knew his father could help. He reconciled with his father, who managed to fix the problem in return for a promise that Jeremy would enroll in his Bible College. Jeremy breezed through the next four years, getting passing grades but never excelling. None of the professors dared give him a failing grade.

Upon graduation, he returned to the church administration

offices. He was given a management position and quickly promoted. Three years after graduation, he became the chancellor of the college and vice president of the church. The church had been stagnating for years. Harold Addison Hart was never a great orator. He had built his organization on the prosperity gospel. He was the first to preach it, and so his ministry grew. But now there were many preaching the same message, and he once again was looking for an edge. Jeremy had the movie star looks and resonant voice that drew people to him. Harold saw that the natural ability of his son could once again put Hart of God Ministries in the spotlight.

Jeremy excelled at his new responsibilities. His charisma and talent were obvious to all who watched the new television show. The ratings and the income soared. Harold began traveling the world, spreading his prosperity gospel, leaving his son to run the television ministry and the college. Jeremy loved the spotlight but did not want to be bogged down with the everyday details of running a multimillion-dollar organization. He wasn't ready to run his father's business. He was equally unprepared to receive the phone call that informed him that his father had died on his way to a black-tie charity event in London, England. The founder and president of Hart of God Ministries had a history of heart disease but had refused to seek medical attention. The massive heart attack in the back of a limo ended his long and prosperous life.

Jeremy stood and walked to a window of the church. Reading through the history of his family had stirred up many long-forgotten feelings. He held the book close to his chest. He knew his father was a clever businessman, but always thought that at his core he really believed what he taught. They never admitted to one another that they did not believe what they preached. Jeremy remembered how he felt when he was around sincere people who lived what they believed. He had forgotten how serene and happy he had been that summer at church camp and wondered now why he hadn't continued down that path.

"So, is this my judgment day?" Jeremy asked.

"More like a question-and-answer session," came the answer.

He stood next to Jeremy. They gazed outside. A gentle breeze brushed over the meadow. Light streamed through the broken panes and openings in the rafters of the abandoned structure.

"Why are we in this old church?"

"I told you I *would go and prepare a place for you.*"

Jeremy looked up at the gaping holes in the roof, and replied, "It says *in my Father's house are many mansions* and this does not seem to fit the bill."

The man was amused that Jeremy wanted to make a point by quoting scripture.

"Haven't you had enough mansions?" He asked.

The preacher had no retort for this. He turned and placed the book on the front pew and stepped up on to the stage, taking a seat at the piano. The young man sat next to him on the bench.

Jeremy used to go into the TV studio and play the piano to relax. This seemed like a perfect opportunity to let music fill his soul. As he was about to place his hands on the keys, they began to play themselves.

It was the most complex mix of melody and composition he had ever heard. The music bathed him in an aura of contentment and unending love. The hauntingly serene music reached that place deep inside where no one had been since the summer he attended Bible camp. He had been sixteen when he surrendered all to a God he didn't understand. He was now coming full circle. Jeremy was being prepared to receive a different version of spirituality than he had been taught.

The song ended and Jeremy began to play. They sat together singing and laughing while banging out old tunes on the upright piano. This sing-along lasted for as long as Jeremy needed.

When the music and laughter subsided they both stood and made their way down to the haggard pew.

"I should be in hell for all the things I have done," Jeremy muttered.

"It looks to me like you have been there for at least the last thirty years," He replied, softly.

Jeremy nodded in agreement and reopened his book of life . . .

The spring of his sixteenth year, Jeremy was attending high school and working at the church administration offices to make extra money. One evening he was walking back home when he remembered he had forgotten his biology book at work. He turned around and started back across the beautifully manicured campus of the Hart of God Ministries. The Bible College and church office complex were filled with flower-laden pathways and immaculate lawns. He loved growing up on these perfect grounds and enjoyed the landscaped oasis that was his hide-and-seek playground.

Swiping his security card at a back door entrance, Jeremy entered the administration office. He hastened up the stairs to the fourth floor. Walking through the empty offices filled with cubicles, he was trying to remember where he had misplaced the textbook. He didn't find it in his cubicle and then remembered he had been in his dad's office at lunch and had taken the book with him. He started down the hallway to the executive suite, past the elaborately furnished reception area, and through the double doors.

The rumors of his father's affair with his secretary had always been dismissed as religious persecution until that moment. Jeremy froze in the doorway, turned abruptly, and ran out of the office. His father chased after him through the darkened offices and corridors. His father finally caught up to him on the set of the television studio and made Jeremy promise never to tell his mother, and his dad promised that he would break it off with Mrs. Perkins.

Crushed and confused, Jeremy came up with a plan. Working in the administration offices, he had access to all the names and email addresses of the financial donors. He composed an email to all parishioners worldwide that stated that he was joining another denomination. Jeremy Addison Hart, the prince of Hart of God Ministries, had snubbed his father and his church.

Jeremy moved out of the family home. His father set him up with a monthly allowance and an apartment in exchange for his silence. That summer he attended a Bible camp. Still hurt and angry, his intention was to embarrass his father, not to get involved with another church. But this camp and its people genuinely lived the lives they professed. The anger and angst of a confused teenager melted away in a log cabin chapel toward the end of that summer, and for the next two years he tried this new way of life. His resolve and determination to do the right thing were constantly challenged, and Jeremy failed to live up to those standards placed upon him.

Page after page, Jeremy read about the incidents of debauchery. With each new paragraph came more and more regret and shame. Knowing he was being watched as he read, he squirmed in his seat. He came to a part in his life that he had tried desperately to forget. Turning the page, he saw an image of a pretty young woman and her child. A chill ran down his spine. Jeremy attempted to close the book but was stopped short.

NINE

"THIS IS some of the work we have to do," He told Jeremy. His hand touched the image on the page, and they were instantly standing in the hallway of a maternity ward. A young pregnant woman was checking in alone and was now being wheeled down a brightly lit hallway. They followed the scene into the delivery room as the young woman told the doctors that the father would be there soon. After sixteen hours of labor, she delivered a beautiful baby boy. She pleaded in vain for the love of her life to come through that door, but the handsome young naval man was nowhere to be found.

Jeremy was stationed in Germany. He had met her at a local tavern not far from the base. The whirlwind romance was filled with passion and promises. Jeremy was content to tell the young girl anything just to get what he wanted. She was thrilled when she learned she was carrying his baby. He promised they would be married, all while trying desperately to figure a way out. When the baby arrived and Jeremy was absent, her love turned into hate. She tracked him down, demanding child support. Jeremy was furious that this had to happen just before he was about to complete his four years in the navy. A couple more weeks and he would have been shipped out. He knew the only way out was to call his father. An emergency meeting of the financial council of elders was called, and they arrived at a sum. A team of lawyers was sent to Germany, and papers were signed insuring her silence. In return, Jeremy was sentenced to a life of servitude within the Hart of God Ministries.

Jeremy looked up from the book and reluctantly asked what had happened to her.

The young girl never married and because of the difficult birth, she was unable to have more children. The years that followed were filled with hatred for herself and Jeremy. The once vibrant and caring woman had turned into a shell where only hate lived. She hit rock bottom when she attempted suicide. Her nine-year-old son wrestled the gun from her trembling hands, stopping a tragedy.

She picked up the pieces and dedicated her life to helping others. She went to college and got her master's degree. The hush money was finally put to good use when she opened the largest shelter for pregnant teens in the country. Her son graduated from college and is happily married. The young couple is expecting twins in the spring.

As Jeremy apologized for his selfish and cowardly behavior, he watched the images and writing on the pages disappear. The realization of what was happening before his eyes overcame him. He had preached a thousand sermons on forgiveness but never had applied it to himself. Jeremy had memorized most of the entire Old and New Testament. His knowledge of scripture was used to wield power and control over those who had looked to him for guidance. He wept as he watched page after page turn white as the driven snow. He pondered his theological training and questions flooding in.

"Where are the Father and the Spirit?"

"I wondered when you were going to ask." He slowly stood and looked toward the rafters.

The largest hole in the roof was just above them. Suddenly two white doves fluttered in, descending onto each of his shoulders. Blinding white light filled the sanctuary. Jeremy stood in awe at the sight before him. He fell to his knees in front of three shining figures.

He squinted as he looked up at the three. At first glance they looked exactly alike. Jeremy looked into their eyes, and it was there that he noticed a subtle difference. The one on the left had a wise and knowing countenance. The one in the middle had compassion in his eyes. The one on the right had the comforting look of a nurturing mother.

The wise and knowing one said, "I breathed into you the breath of life."

The one in the middle said, "This is my son in whom I am well pleased."

The one on the right said, "I am with you always."

The windows shook and the floor rumbled as their words filled the tiny church. A cleansing breeze swept through the windows and doorway, and once again a lone figure stood in front of the trembling preacher. Jeremy looked up at the dark-haired man with the amiable eyes. He pulled Jeremy to his feet.

"Any other questions?" He asked.

"No, thank you, that was enough for a while," Jeremy whispered.

This brought a huge laugh. He patted Jeremy on the back, then walked toward the open door at the back of the church. Jeremy followed. They made their way down the broken steps. Jeremy noticed the majestic oak tree across the meadow standing guard over the area. They walked to the left around the building.

He stopped and turned toward Jeremy. "Are you ready to start fixing up this place?"

Jeremy looked beyond Him toward a pile of freshly cut lumber. Sawhorses, ladders, hammers, saws, and two leather tool belts sat on the grass in front of him.

"I have no idea how to build a church," Jeremy said sheepishly.

"Well, I have to agree with you there," He said with a wink.

Jeremy smiled, realizing the irony of his statement.

The seasoned carpenter tossed a tool belt to Jeremy and said, "Let's get started!"

Jeremy fumbled with the tool belt, eventually strapping it on.

Unrolling a scroll, He explained His ideas and vision for the old country church. He asked Jeremy his thoughts and invited his ideas into the discussion.

Jeremy felt a sense of belonging as he looked at the plans and drawings. He was being included in the decisions. Although Jeremy had never built a home or even picked up a hammer, he did have creative ideas and vision. He suggested a few things and watched in awe as the plans and drawings transformed to fit his ideas.

They placed a wooden ladder against the side of the church. Jeremy was surprised he could lift the freshly cut plywood as he scampered up the ladder. They repaired the holes on the roof. Working side by side over the sound of hammers, Jeremy was once again asked to account for his life.

He noticed his red bound book open on the shingles in front of him. As he hammered the wood into place, a light breeze rustled the pages. A new page lay open in front of him. On the page was an image of a man in his late fifties with a weathered face and the uniform of a janitor. Jeremy stopped hammering as he gazed at the image. He noticed the logo on the man's uniform shirt was that of Hart of God Ministries. *Ronald* was embroidered above the left pocket.

Jeremy's companion reached across Jeremy's arm and touched the image on the page.

Instantly, they were standing on a sidewalk in the middle of the beautifully manicured grounds of the church and college campus. Jeremy knew every inch of that campus and immediately recognized where they were. A door to the administration office flew open and out came Jeremy Addison Hart and his entourage. They watched as the group hurriedly walked toward them on their way to the television studio. The enamored staff surrounded the handsome preacher, trying desperately to tend to his every need.

Ronald Brewster was a dedicated and loyal member of the church. His undying love for Jeremy and the church was obvious to all who knew him. Ronald was a hardworking man who felt it an honor to be able to work for the church he so passionately adored. His dream was to someday be able to preach the gospel like his idol Jeremy Addison Hart. He enrolled in the church college, taking night classes and working on the custodial staff during the day.

The entourage whisked their boss to the television station. He had been asked to do a live interview on CNN about his church and his version of the gospel. As usual, he was running late. His assistants were trying to prep him for the questions he would be asked as they hurried across the campus.

Jeremy vaguely remembered that day, but could not figure out why they were watching this moment of his life. They stood inside the television studio watching a younger version of him approaching the lobby, trying to down a cup of coffee while listening to last-minute instructions from his staff.

Ronald had been early that morning and was proud of himself because he had already cleaned the television studio and offices, and was finishing cleaning and waxing the marble floor of the lobby. He was thrilled to see Jeremy and his group approach. Maybe this morning he would be noticed. Maybe Mr. Hart would compliment him on his efforts and hard work.

The glass double doors were flung open for the self-proclaimed apostle as he hurried into the lobby. Ronald cringed, aware the freshly waxed floor would be slippery. Before he could warn Jeremy, Ronald watched in horror as his favorite preacher slipped and fell on the hard marble. The coffee Jeremy had been carrying in his hand spilled all over his silk tie and tailor-made suit.

His staff helped an embarrassed, but otherwise unharmed, Jeremy to his feet.

Jeremy looked at the man in the janitorial uniform and saw the floor-buffing machine and mop behind him. He waved his finger in Ronald's face.

"I am about to go on live TV, and you have made me ruin my new suit!"

He continued, calling Ronald an idiot and worthless. His staff squirmed as he screamed insults at his humble employee.

Then came the words, "You are fired!"

With that, the arrogant preacher ordered security guards to escort Ronald from the premises immediately. Jeremy and his minions scurried through the lobby with the echoing sounds of Ronald crying and pleading for his job in their ears.

TEN

WHILE JEREMY HELPED REPAIR the roof he was told what had become of Ronald Brewster. Ronald's weathered, smiling face stared back at Jeremy from the open page. The book of life bounced slightly with each strike of their hammers.

The apprentice listened to the master carpenter as he recalled the next 12 years of the former janitor's life. Ronald Brewster was emotionally and spiritually crushed that day in the lobby. His spiritual mentor had humiliated him and left him unemployed. The college refused to let him continue his studies, and it was suggested he find another place to worship. He was devastated. His belief system had been turned upside down. Ronald quit going to church and gave up on his dream of preaching the gospel. For years he drifted from job to job. He was no longer capable of propping up his lost, dejected soul; his marriage soured, and his wife of thirty years left him.

Sitting alone in his house, Ronald reasoned with himself. How could he have given this much power to another person? Why did he let his marriage and his faith just pass him by? His wife had always wanted him to try again. She told him Jeremy Addison Hart was a bad example of what true spirituality really was. Her pleadings finally made sense. Sitting there in the dark of his empty home, he cried out two words: "Help me." The phone rang within seconds. His next-door neighbor Gene was calling from the hospital. He was frantic. He explained to his friend that he and his wife Lisa had been out to dinner when she had collapsed. She was in intensive care. Gene asked Ronald to come to the hospital.

Ronald grabbed his keys off the cluttered dining room table and stumbled from his dark and lonely house to help his friend. On the drive to the hospital, he had time to reflect on what Gene and Lisa meant to him. Ronald and Gene, Lisa and Tina, two sets of best friends. Although Ronald had become increasingly withdrawn over the last few years, Gene had always been there to commiserate. Lisa and Tina drew closer as Ronald became increasingly bitter. It was hard for Gene and Lisa to watch their friends' marriage slowly die, but Ronald wouldn't listen. His self-pity and righteous indignation continued to erode the marriage. Now he was without his precious wife Tina, and Gene was in fear of losing Lisa.

As Ronald entered the intensive-care waiting room, a tired and fearful-looking Gene stood to hug him. Ronald held his old friend, trying to reassure him. Gene said he had to get back into the room with Lisa but wanted Ron to stay at the hospital. Ronald promised he would stay as long as Gene needed him to. He watched his old friend hurry out of the room and back to his wife.

Ronald went to the chapel. He had not been in a church or prayed for many years. Walking into the small chapel, he noticed his estranged wife lighting a candle. She heard the door and immediately turned to see her husband standing in a church for the first time in twelve years.

They embraced in the small aisle, not saying a word. The flicker of the candle in the dimly lit room cast shadows on their worried faces. Ronald wondered what had compelled him to come to the chapel. He told himself it was because he thought she would be there, but he knew in his heart that there was more to it. They sat quietly and Ronald found himself praying. He asked that Lisa would recover, and then he began to weep. Twelve years of anger at God, and everyone else, poured out of him. His estranged wife held his head on her shoulder.

Lisa did recover from the mild stroke. Within a month, she was back in her garden working on her flowers, but now Gene was beside her. Tina moved home with Ronald to start a new chapter in their lives. Ronald had reopened his heart and was willing to listen to the possibility of a spiritual life.

Jeremy stopped hammering. "All that pain and wasted time because of my actions."

"You were the catalyst, but you were not the cause," came the answer from the young carpenter. He looked at Jeremy and said, "Ronald was putting you before me. That was his choice. What you did to him was deplorable, but what he did with it was his choice. You were so wrapped up in being Jeremy Addison Hart that you never once considered that your actions have real and lasting consequences."

As Jeremy said that he was sorry, he noticed the page with Ronald's face turn white, and then a light breeze turned the page.

The roof had been repaired and shingled. As they descended the ladder, Jeremy felt a sense of accomplishment he had never before experienced.

"Let's take a break," said the Carpenter.

They walked toward the wise old oak tree in the meadow in front of the church. In its expansive shade, Jeremy noticed his book lying next to a picnic basket on a blanket. They sat and leaned against the mighty trunk. Birds joyously welcomed them with songs and chirps. Jeremy watched as his companion looked up into the tree, mimicking every bird exactly. It was a wonder to watch Him have a conversation with all His feathered friends.

"What does my father think of all of this?" Jeremy asked. The smile on the young carpenter's face quickly faded as He dropped His gaze from the trees.

Tears welled in His eyes as He looked across the meadow.

"Did I say something wrong?" Jeremy asked.

"No, it's perfectly logical that you would wonder about him. He was on his way to a charity event in London when he arrived," He said.

"I remember getting the call. It was quite a shock," Jeremy said. The birds filled the moments of awkward silence that followed. Finally, his new friend broke the silence.

"Your dad arrived much as you did, all puffed up and angry. He too had a pretty high opinion of himself. We talked at length about his life. I gave him his book, but he would not open it. He argued with me and tried to justify his actions. Although he never opened his book, he was still forced to look at that which he denied."

"Eventually, he was given a choice to stay and acknowledge his actions or have his book of life burned, thus eliminating any possibility of reconciliation."

Tears rolled down His cheeks as He told Jeremy that his father had been stricken from the book of life. "When a soul dies, there is a sickening howl that echoes through the valleys of heaven. All the choirs, the birds, the trees, the flowers, everything you see and hear cries out for the one who is lost. I remember standing at the precipice between eternity and oblivion as the last remnant of my son, Harold, slipped through my fingers."

Jeremy sat, stunned at what he had just heard. His father was gone for all eternity. He wondered how anyone could choose to be vanquished rather than admit his or her faults. All the memories of his father were quickly disappearing, and he realized it would soon be as if he had never existed. A cold chill ran over him.

"Goodbye, Dad," he sobbed, as the final awareness of his father's essence drifted from his consciousness.

They ate in silence under the shade of the ancient tree. Jeremy felt a sense of great loss, but could not quite remember why. The longer they sat sharing a meal, the better he felt. The quiet companionship soothed and comforted him.

The book was opened again. This time Jeremy had to acknowledge his unfaithfulness to his wife, Sheryl. He had met her at college and begged her to marry him upon graduation. She was a beautiful young woman, and Jeremy felt she would keep him on the straight and narrow path. He needed her acceptance desperately, but knew in his heart he would never be able to keep his wedding vows. Time after time over the years he had pleaded for her forgiveness, and Sheryl had forgiven him. He now asked the Carpenter for His forgiveness, and all those pages turned white and disappeared.

Every lie Jeremy had ever told, even those he had told himself, were all written in the book. Page after page stared back at him. The sheer volume of untruthful statements, phone calls, letters, emails, and private thoughts that filled this section of the book astonished him. It had never occurred to him that even the untruthful things we tell ourselves would be considered a lie.

"The lies you told yourself were the most damaging of all. All the actions you took were based on those little stories and justifications you had created to soothe your conscience. The longer you did it, the more elaborate the stories had to become. You got to the place where you believed your own garbage."

With his misdeeds erased from the record, it was time to look at the positive things. Jeremy watched as the book was snatched from his hand. A broad smile came across the face of his newfound friend as He began to describe at length the good things that Jeremy had accomplished in his life. Pride and joy flashed in His eyes as he began to recite these assets on the ledger.

He placed the book under His arm. "Come on, let's go work on the church."

Jeremy followed as they walked past the front of the church with its broken stairs and around the back. They strapped on their tool belts. He noticed there were boards cut to the exact specifications for the front steps lying on the grass. The smell of fresh-cut lumber filled the air as they picked up the boards and headed for the front of the church.

The apprentice listened as the carpenter started to tell stories. He recalled the time when Jeremy was seven years old. There was a dog named Rascal that lived in the neighborhood. The church and college had yet to buy up all the old houses and expand. Across the street from the original church building was a row of houses that Jeremy used to walk by on his way to the park. Rascal was a mixture of this and that, which made him an adorable ball of fur that welcomed any passerby.

Rascal was chained in the front yard of the ugliest house on the block. The home was a two-story monument to neglect. Behind the rusted chain-link fence, Rascal ran back and forth in the dirt of what once was a nice yard. His fur was matted and dirty, and his food and water bowl were rarely filled. Every time Jeremy would come by he would bring snacks. Rascal would wag and wiggle and devour every bit of the treats. Jeremy would reach through the holes in the mangled fence and pet his furry friend.

One summer morning he was riding his bike to the park to play and decided he would stop and see Rascal. As he approached, he noticed something was wrong. Rascal was limping and had a gash on the top of his head. Jeremy dropped his bike and opened the creaking gate to help the puppy. Rascal slowly approached with his ears down and his eyes half-open. Jeremy knew that the dog never left the yard, so this had to have been the work of his owner. As Jeremy was trying to tend to the shivering puppy, his suspicions were confirmed. The front door opened. There on the front porch stood a screaming half-drunk hulk of a man.

"Get away from my dog, you little brat!" he slurred.

Jeremy jumped up and ran out of the gate. The puppy cowered against the fence as his master waved a lead pipe over his head. Jeremy raced away from the scene, determined to return that night and rescue Rascal.

Jeremy quietly laid down his bike and approached the shabby house. Moonlight illuminated the front yard. He eased the front gate open, making sure there was no squeak. He removed his backpack and took out some rubber gloves, a small camping shovel, a thermos of hot water, and some fishing line.

Picking up the little dog's poop, he started to stack a pile at the bottom of the front steps. Standing back, he smiled. The pile had become a foot-high mound. He tied the fishing line to both ends of the pillars on either side of the stairs. Jeremy unscrewed the top of the thermos and poured the hot water on the mound, turning it into a soupy mess. Avoiding the mess he'd created, he crept up the front steps, pounded on the front door, and then ran into the front yard.

Rascal began barking from inside the house. A light flicked on and the front door was flung open. The drunken, screaming man lunged across his front porch. The fishing line caught him between his ankles and knees, sending him flying face first into the slippery stinking mound at the bottom of the steps. Rascal bolted out the front door, leaping over the sputtering drunk and into the arms of his rescuer. Jeremy raced to his bike with Rascal shivering under his arm. A lead pipe swished over his head, clanking on the street in front of them. The swearing and yelling faded as they rounded the curve under the cover of night.

ELEVEN

THE STORY WAS NOW BEING INTERRUPTED by rollicking laughter. They had stopped building and were both sitting on the steps of the church doubled over holding their stomachs. As the wheezing and cackling subsided, a description of the poop-soaked man once again sent them into fits of laughter.

"Who do you think gave you that diabolical plan?" said the Carpenter through His laughter.

Jeremy looked surprised. "I always thought that was a pretty sophisticated plan for a seven-year old!" He paused. "What happened to that guy?"

The Carpenter looked at him with a twinkle in His eye.

"He was arrested for animal cruelty from an anonymous phone tip."

They went back to building the stairs. Jeremy was really enjoying what the master carpenter was patiently teaching him. It occurred to him that he had a knack for construction. The Carpenter continued reminding him of things in his life of which He was particularly proud, and the book would suddenly open to that page. As they built the railings, the book opened to an image he had long forgotten - Lakeside Summer Camp.

The camp was set on a peninsula of a large lake. Pine and white birch trees surrounded the log cabin retreat. Jeremy was an angry young man who had signed up for camp as a way to escape his home life. His cynicism and teenage angst automatically isolated him from the rest of the campers.

Ricky Nolder was a skinny, gangly kid who had trouble making friends. Jeremy met him the day they were all learning how to fish. Ricky got his line tangled up in the trees, and the ridicule from others began. The instructors and counselors noticed as Jeremy stood up for Ricky. From that moment on, Ricky and Jeremy were fast friends. The two loners were getting involved in their summer camp experience. Jeremy always made sure Ricky was picked for any team sports, and Ricky always saved Jeremy a place in line at the dining hall.

Wherever the two of them went, Ricky was constantly telling Jeremy about his faith. On this one subject the awkwardly shy kid transformed into a confident and articulate spokesman. This would have normally infuriated Jeremy, but for some reason Ricky had a way of presenting his views that made Jeremy listen. His humble and optimistic approach to life despite his physical shortcomings always impressed Jeremy.

By the end of that summer, the angry and cynical Jeremy surrendered in a log cabin chapel with Ricky by his side. They exchanged addresses and promised to keep in touch. Ricky wrote Jeremy a letter a week for many months. Jeremy replied twice. Then the letters came once every two weeks and then not at all. The skeptical side of Jeremy thought that Ricky had just gotten bored with writing, but that didn't seem like the Ricky he knew. He got permission to call Ricky and was shocked when the grieving mother told him that her little Ricky had died of cancer. He had been diagnosed with an aggressive form of cancer that was already too far along to treat. He had decided that he would spend his last summer at summer camp.

She told him that Ricky talked of him often and was so grateful to have had a friend like him.

Jeremy was kneeling as he pounded nails into the new front stoop of the church. The book lay open in front of him with an image of two childhood friends standing next to a bus. He remembered that picture being taken on their last day of camp, as Ricky was getting ready to leave. He began to realize that Ricky had been his one true friend. His whole life he was surrounded by people who said they loved him, but he knew it was not true. This young man wanted nothing from him but his friendship.

Regret began to set in. He realized he had basically forgotten Ricky. He reached behind him to pick up another board, and there stood Ricky handing one to him.

"Ricky!" Jeremy yelled.

The two old friends embraced, laughing and patting each other on the back. Ricky and Jeremy picked up where they had left off, as if no time had elapsed. They made plans to go fishing soon, and then Ricky joked with Jeremy, telling him to get back to work. Jeremy watched his old friend as he walked down the gravel road beside the church. Waving to his friend, he watched until Ricky disappeared around the bend.

The carpenter stood next to Jeremy.

"Some people were only in your life for a season. You did well by befriending Ricky. It was my hope that he would have affected you in a more profound and lasting way while you were on earth. Now you can spend eternity with your old friend. I think his example is one you could still take to heart."

They finished the front stoop and started replacing the window frames and glass. With that finished, they moved on to scraping the old paint off and painting the exterior of the ancient country church. With paint-smeared clothes, they stood back admiring the now-gleaming white structure.

The entire time they were working the book was always present. The apprentice listened to the master carpenter as He brought up positive aspects of Jeremy's life. They brought the wood inside the church and began building and repairing the pews. Jeremy started asking questions about life, creation, theology, and religion.

"Where did you go for three days and three nights? You did not ascend to the Father, so where did you go?"

The master carpenter stopped carving the intricate design on the back of a pew. A mournful look swept across His face as He began.

"As you probably know, the universe is always expanding. Beyond that, there is a nothingness that is hard to describe. It is a dark and hollow place. The Father and the Spirit did not reside with me for the first time in all eternity. The first day I took on the transgressions of the past. They ate at me like a ravenous animal. The second day I added the sins of the present, and it was even more painful and sickening. The third day all the trespasses of the future were heaped upon me. I cried out for Abba, but could not be heard. I became all the perversion, hate, anger, and fear for all. I embodied the hopelessness and guilt for every human being. I screamed as the filth overtook me. The agony I felt on Golgotha was nothing compared to those three days and nights. All the murders, rapes, wars, and innermost depravity of all mankind enveloped me.

"At the end of the third night I cried out from the deepest canyon of degradation. My pleading screams thundered across the void until they reached the Father. The heavens rumbled with the sound of the stone being rolled away, and I knew I would soon be reunited. I remember running to them across the floor of the throne room as the three became one again. An explosion of bright light emanated from the throne of grace, signaling the success of complete reconciliation between God and mankind. The billions of angels and all the universe joined in a triumphant chorus as we joyously clung to one another."

He looked at Jeremy who had an awestruck look on his face. "Now we celebrate every time a child decides to follow this way of life," He said.

"I bet you had bets against me!" Jeremy joked.

They laughed together as they continued to carve the pews. Questions and answers continued. Jeremy wondered why we needed a church in heaven. The answer was that some people feel the need to gather and celebrate, and we want to accommodate that need. He asked about organized religion. The carpenter answered with a smirk on his face,

"When I see an organized religion, I will let you know."

He wondered about all the dinosaurs and man-like creatures that were on earth before man. The answer was that He is always trying new things, and it was not yet the season for mankind.

The pews were finished and put in place. They swept up the sawdust and cleaned the hardwood floors. The hymnals were picked up and placed in the backs of the pews. The windows were scrubbed clean and a newly built pulpit was put in place. They stood at the back of the church and examined their work.

Jeremy turned to the master builder.

"This will be a great place for me to start preaching."

There was no response.

He continued, "I think that I just needed to realize that it was not about the size of the sanctuary. It was about the message."

Still, no response.

Jeremy looked at his friend. He noticed a smile on His face.

"What?" Jeremy asked.

The carpenter asked Jeremy to have a seat on one of the new polished pews.

He looked into Jeremy's eyes.

"We did not do all this work on this church for you."

"I know. It's for the people. This will be a place where I can really preach, instead of putting on a show for my own gratification," Jeremy said.

The carpenter continued.

"I really had someone else in mind. I just wanted you to help me get it ready."

Jeremy was shocked.

"You don't want me to preach here?"

"Your days of preaching ended on that purple carpet in your television studio. I wanted you to help me prepare this church for its new pastor, Ronald Brewster. Ronald will be here very soon. He never got his chance to realize his dream of becoming a pastor. Although he came back to his faith, he never got his chance to go back to school and grow into what he was meant to do. Your former janitor will be the pastor, and you will be the caretaker of this church. I have taught you how to build and repair this building, so now all you have to do is keep it clean. There will be four services every day, so that should keep you busy. I built you a fine home out behind the church next to the parsonage," He explained.

Jeremy sat back in the pew and started to snicker. He expected to feel anger and jealousy, but instead he felt total love and acceptance. They stood together and began walking out of the church. They stepped off the newly built steps and toward the wise old oak tree. In its shade, He turned to Jeremy and smiled. In His hand He had the book with Jeremy's name on its spine.

He closed the book.

"Well done, my good and faithful servant," He said.

He gave Jeremy a big bear hug.

"This spot under the oak tree will always be our spot. Whenever you want to talk to me, I will meet you right here. I have a big celebration planned for you down in the city. Let me go see if everything is ready, and I will come pick you up on my horse."

With that, He turned and walked down the gravel road past the pristine white church. As if on cue, the bell clanged from the steeple tower, and a flock of birds fluttered off the rooftop to follow Him as He disappeared around the bend.

TWELVE

HIS BROTHER'S KEEPER

"Judge not, that ye be not judged." Matthew 7:1

THE SMOKE and flames of the surrounding War Between the States obscured the church at Shiloh. Kenny was ducking his head from the gunfire while hiding behind a fallen log. When he was loaded and ready to fire, he would lift his head and shoot at any blue uniform he could see. The screaming death that surrounded him was a low hum to his ears. The many days and nights of little sleep and constant gore had numbed him. Fear had become his constant companion. It was the only thing he could rely on. His friends were dead and his commanding officer lay dying at his feet.

As the smoke cleared, he lifted his rifle and took aim. A Yankee soldier was running across a grassy clearing when Kenny spotted him. The pulling of the trigger coincided with the realization of who the soldier was. Kenny screamed out his brother Billy's name just as he saw his brother collapse. He hurtled the fallen log and started running through the deluge. He dodged soldiers involved in hand-to-hand combat as he hurried toward his brother.

Kenny was determined to reach Billy, as he shot two soldiers and stabbed three more with his bayonet on his way to his brother's side. He ran across the battlefield as a shot rang out to his left. He felt a white-hot pain in his side, which slowed his pace. He knew he was now vulnerable but continued running. The second shot came from beyond the trees. The bullet entered just under his ribcage. Kenny stumbled as he began to choke on his own blood. He collapsed at Billy's side. He grabbed his brother's coat and turned his face toward him.

Kenny looked at the death mask of his brother as the horror of war trampled over them. Clinging hard to Billy and survival, Kenny felt his life slipping from his grasp. Waves of quiet and calamity ebbed and flowed over him. Memories of hide-and-seek and building a tree house with Billy rushed through his mind. He could feel the slumber of death overtake him. He lay his head on the shoulder of the enemy, his brother in a war where nobody won.

Kenny opened his eyes and immediately started looking for Billy. He yelled out to him, but no one answered. The carnage of war seemed to have passed. He thought about his rifle and started panicking. He had been shot and was vulnerable to attack. Without his rifle, he was a sitting duck. He figured someone must have moved him to safety, because he was now lying under an old oak tree. The Shiloh church was no longer there. There was no smoke or gunfire, just a quiet meadow surrounded by trees. All the dead soldiers on both sides were gone as well. That thought brought back the realization that he had taken his brother's life. He dropped his head into his hands and began to weep.

He felt a tap on his shoulder and abruptly looked up. In front of him stood a young black man with a handkerchief in his hand.

"Sometimes it feels good to just sit down and cry," the man said.

Kenny was startled and backed against the tree.

"Get away from me!" Kenny screamed.

"My name is Potter," he said, undaunted by Kenny's attitude.

Kenny stuck out his chin and gritted his teeth. "You are not allowed to speak unless spoken to!"

Potter frowned. "Why do you say that?"

"Because you are just a Nig- "Kenny clutched his throat, coughing.

"There is no cursing here," Potter said.

Kenny's tongue swelled, and his throat became bone dry. He was unable to utter a sound.

The silence was broken by Kenny gasping and hacking. "What happened to my voice?" he sputtered, stroking his throat.

"Seems like you choked on some hatred," Potter said.

Kenny dismissed his comment.

"Did you bring me here?" he asked.

Potter put his thumbs in his suspenders. "I surely did. You were lying on the battlefield, praying for Jesus to forgive you. It looked to me like you needed saving, so I brought you here."

"Where is my brother?" Kenny asked.

"You mean that Union soldier you were clinging to?"

"Yes! What happened to him?

"He is in a better place," Potter answered.

Kenny hung his head.

"But then, so are you."

Kenny felt bewildered. "What do you mean?"

Potter pointed to Kenny's uniform. "You have bullet holes in the side and front, but no blood."

Kenny unbuttoned his coat and reached inside. He knew he had been shot in the side and under his ribcage, but there was no evidence of it. Kenny looked up at the young black man dressed in a faded red shirt and old pants held up by suspenders. He had no shoes on his feet.

"Did you learn some doctorin' from your master? Is that why I don't have any wounds?" the Confederate soldier asked.

"Let's just say I know something about healing."

"It must have taken a long time to fix me up. I have to return to my unit," Kenny insisted.

"Time is no longer something you need to worry about. As far as the war goes, your part is over. The battle at Shiloh church was eventually won by the Union army, but not until it took upwards of twenty-four thousand lives on both sides," Potter said.

Kenny stood. He looked the young black man straight in the eye. "We may have lost the battle, but we will win the war!"

Potter shook his head.

"There is never a winner in war, only a victor. The Union army was victorious in the War between the States."

Kenny did not want to believe this. He was shocked and felt himself lean back against the trunk of the mighty oak tree.

"Where do you get your information?" Kenny demanded.

Potter smiled. His kind eyes looked at the young recruit.

"The battle of Shiloh church happened in 1862, but the war ended in 1865. You were taken away from the conflict long before it ended."

Kenny tried to wrap his mind around what he had just heard. "Have I been in a coma for three years?"

"You have been gone less than five minutes from your physical existence, but the war rages on for another three years," Potter explained.

The things he was hearing from this stranger sounded crazy. He remembered choking on his own blood and the feeling of inevitable death overtaking him. He recalled the moment that comes to all who die, that instant when you surrender to death's grasp. The last pleadings of forgiveness mixed with memories of his life before all went black.

Potter watched as Kenny tried to reconcile that memory with his current reality. If he had succumbed to death, why was he still alive? He hated himself for feeling gratitude toward Potter.

"Why did you save me from death?" Kenny asked.

"I never said I did. What I said was you seemed like you needed saving," Potter said.

Kenny remembered the pain of his wounds and realized they had vanished. A glimmer of realization slowly began to creep into his thoughts. He remembered gasping his last breath and praying that there was something on the other side. The question came to the front of his mind, but he was afraid to utter it.

"The answer is yes. Kenneth Jordan Wilson has transformed into spirit and is no longer a part of the earthly realm," Potter said.

"You mean I am dead?"

"You have been changed from mortal into immortal. There is no death here."

Kenny's eyes grew wide as he thought what this must mean.

"If I died and you are standing here, then that can only mean one thing," Kenny said.

Potter tilted his head and asked, "What's that?"

"I must be in hell. They don't let Negroes into heaven," Kenny answered.

Potter reared his head back and laughed uproariously. The birds in the tree above them joined in as they fluttered out of the leaves.

"Do you think it's funny to be in hell?" Kenny asked.

Potter had his hands on his knees, shaking his head as he composed himself.

"I think it's funny that you think only white people can be in heaven," Potter snorted.

Kenny looked around. The sunless blue sky and the wildflowers in the meadow were more vivid than he had ever seen. The feeling of peace and order that permeated every living thing was in stark contrast to his concept of eternal damnation.

"Is this heaven?" Kenny asked.

"Heaven, yes!" Potter joked.

"I was always taught that Negroes couldn't be saved, so I thought they all went to hell when they died," Kenny said.

Potter placed his hand on Kenny's shoulder.

"Well, you have a lot to learn. That is why I came to meet you."

Kenny looked at Potter skeptically. "God sent you to meet me? I don't believe it! I need to find the pearly gates and the angels. I need to ask forgiveness for shooting my brother, Billy, so I can enter into my eternal rest."

He pushed Potter aside and started off across the meadow in search of God.

A booming voice that seemed to come from everywhere stopped him in his tracks.

"It is appointed for every man to die and then the judgment."

The ground shook at the resonance of the voice. He looked back to see Potter sitting at a table with two chairs. Kenny slowly turned around and headed back toward the oak tree.

"Have a seat," Potter said.

Kenny reluctantly took the chair opposite Potter.

"Before you go running off in search of God, I think I must tell you that you will never find him that way. I have been in these woods for a long time and have found that without a guide and a clear direction, you will always be lost," Potter said.

"Do you know the way? Are you my guide?" Kenny asked.

"I am the way. You will not find Him without me."

Kenny was still cynical. "Why would God send a black man who hasn't even been given shoes to guide me?"

Potter smiled patiently. "I have no shoes, to show you I walk in humility."

Kenny looked down at Potter's scarred feet. He noticed his hands had similar scars and wondered if they had come at the hands of a former master in another life.

Potter seemed to read his thoughts.

"The scars are from the children that did not know who I was."

Kenny did not understand this strange man, but felt compelled to listen. The anxious rebel soldier looked across the table. "You have shown others how to get there?"

Potter nodded.

"Do you have a map book? In our regiment, there was always a guide with a book of maps. We would have been lost without him."

Potter smiled and nodded. "It is the same way here."

He asked Kenny to check his uniform pocket. Kenny reached in and pulled out a tattered book. It had a compass insignia on the front cover. On the spine, it read: Kenneth Jordan Wilson.

Kenny snorted. He gazed at Potter with disdain. "So even up here you are given the job of a servant to be my guide."

Potter indulged the arrogant Confederate. "Yes, I guess that is right, Kenny. Let's get started."

Kenny stood.

"Where are you going?" Potter asked.

Kenny sat back down. "You gave me the map book, so let's get a move on."

Potter shook his head. "This book will lead you to truth and that is where God is."

THIRTEEN

KENNY FROWNED at his guide and opened the book. The front page had his name on it.

"This is your book of life, Kenny. This journey through your life will ultimately get you where you want to go, if you so choose. It is up to you what direction you will take," Potter said.

Kenny opened the first page and saw the small homestead where he had been born. He had been the last of three children, William, Anna, and Kenny Wilson. He smiled at the memories and then remembered his older brother. He looked up from the book.

"Will I ever see him again?"

"Like I said, that is up to you," Potter answered.

Kenny's father was a resourceful man. He started out on fifty acres of land and a small homestead. He grew his fortune to a thousand acres. He was a cotton farmer whose empire had grown on the backs of hundreds of slaves. The entirety of his wealth could be directly attributed to slavery. The Wilson children grew up in opulence. The mansion Kenny grew up in was filled with winding staircases and crystal chandeliers. He always thought the slaves were appreciative of their station. Kenny thought his father, Sebastian Wilson, was a good slave owner.

He turned the page and saw the image of a small black boy named Jeremiah. Jeremiah was four years younger than he. Since Kenny was the youngest of the Wilsons, he loved having a playmate that he could boss around for a change. He recalled the many hours they would play in the barns and pastures of the Wilson estate. Kenny kept secret from his family that he felt Jeremiah was more a friend than a slave. Kenny ran his fingers across the image and wondered what had happened to Jeremiah. He recalled the summer morning when he ran down the hill in back of the mansion. Across a large gully stood the shantytown that was home to hundreds of slave families. Kenny and Jeremiah would meet near the bushes and play for as long as they could. Jeremiah did not dare be gone too long, and Kenny knew he only had a small amount of time before his mother would worry. They ran and played in their imaginations, blotting out the divided world around them.

This morning was different. When Kenny arrived at their meeting place, Jeremiah was nowhere to be found. He looked over the top of the gully into the large collection of shacks just beyond the trees. He heard women crying and wailing and wondered what had happened to his friend. He waited for as long as he could and then scampered back up the hill, never to hear from his friend again. Looking at the image of young Jeremiah on the page brought back the pain of loss. Young Kenny had cried himself to sleep for weeks, mourning the loss of his secret friend.

He looked up from the book, angry and restless, and sneered at Potter, "Whatever happened to that little brat? He probably got what he deserved."

"Hating is a lot easier than feeling. We will come back to this when you are ready," Potter said.

Kenny stared at Potter and turned the page. His young life was filled with memories of large parties where carriages lined up in front of his house. He would watch the adults, dressed in their festive best, parade across the massive front porch. He was taught that a heavenly father that loved the old south and all its traditions blessed him and his brother and sister. The disparity between the shanties and the mansions were understood to be God's will.

The older Kenny grew, the more entitled he became. In his sixteenth year, Kenny decided he would pull a prank on the neighboring estate by stealing their carriages. He and his friends crept onto the property of the Jensen farm and waited in the shadows until nightfall. The Jensen family had five daughters and was one of the prominent families in the area. The head of the Jensen clan was one Theodore Jensen. He would never let his beautiful daughters participate in the dances or social gatherings. This infuriated all the young men in the area, and they decided to strike back. When the coast seemed to be clear, they came out of hiding and started running toward the stables. Joseph Peters, Lewis Bonner, and Kenny Wilson were best friends. They reached the barn and stopped to catch their breath. It was hard to run and giggle at the same time.

"Old man Jensen's gonna have a surprise tomorrow morning!" Joseph whispered.

Kenny and Lewis tried to suppress their laughter as they snuck into the barn.

Mr. Jensen prided himself on his two new carriages. They had been hand-made by a company in San Francisco and shipped by train to his estate. They were then assembled and put on display in the recent Fourth of July parade. Jensen had all his daughters and his wife in the two carriages as he proudly rode through the middle of town.

The boys quickly and quietly hooked up the horses and opened the barn doors. Just as they were about to take off, two young slaves entered the barn. Tobias and Elijah were responsible for the stables and were not about to let this happen. They both yelled as the boys whipped the reins. As the carriages took off, Tobias and Elijah ran after them. They each jumped onto a carriage and tried to stop the youngsters. The strength of the grown men was too much for these children. The commotion awoke the Jensen household as the carriages went whisking by the front porch. Tobias and Elijah overpowered the three pranksters and threw them from the moving carriages. As the two slaves attempted to slow the horses, old man Jensen appeared on his veranda. He saw his two slaves racing through the night with his precious carriages. He immediately rang the bell that hung from his upper balcony. Within minutes, he had summoned his men to retrieve the escaping slaves and his carriages.

The three boys lay in a ditch, bruised and battered, watching Jensen's men race after Tobias and Elijah. The two were apprehended within minutes. The boys watched as Tobias and Elijah tried to explain that they were trying to save the carriages from being stolen. This explanation got a big laugh from Jensen's men. Old man Jensen was waiting on his front porch when they returned. The two slaves were dragged in front of him. They pleaded their case, but to no avail.

"No slave tries to escape with my property! Beat them but do not kill my prize bulls!" Jensen yelled.

The three boys watched in silence as Tobias and Elijah were dragged off into the night. The three boys ran as fast as they could in the opposite direction.

Kenny closed the book and placed it on the table. He couldn't look at Potter.

"Do you think that was just?" Potter asked.

"If we had spoken up, we would have been in big trouble," Kenny justified.

"Those fine young men were beaten to death because of something you did. The trouble you would have faced in your spoiled lives was nothing compared to what they received. Don't you agree?" Potter stared at him.

Kenny shifted in his chair and looked out at the meadow in front of him. He wondered what had happened to Tobias and Elijah. He was surprised that he was even considering their fate. A tinge of remorse started to creep in as he sat taking in the serenity of his surroundings. This feeling of regret quickly turned to anger.

"What does this have to do with finding my way to God?" Kenny asked.

"Absolutely everything, Kenny," Potter said.

"We were just kids and that is the way it was. If the war is over and the Confederacy lost, then they probably went free and lived great lives. So, what is the big deal?"

Potter looked over Kenny's shoulder at the oak tree. Kenny turned to see what Potter was looking at. Tobias and Elijah were leaning on either side of the tree. Kenny's mouth dropped open. The two strong men were dressed in suits, straight out of the 1800s. They strode over to the table. "Hello, Kenny," they said in unison.

Tobias said, "That night we were dragged off was the last night we had on earth. Old man Jensen ordered the men not to kills us but they went too far. They dropped our bodies off in front of the shanty-town for our families to find."

Elijah moved forward. "I know that your father and Jensen had a good relationship. If you would have stepped forward, he would have believed you."

Kenny looked up at these handsome, well-dressed men. He knew he had never seen them after that night, but never really wanted to know why.

"It was Jensen, not me! Why aren't you talking to him?" Kenny pleaded.

The two looked at Potter.

Potter said, "I think it would be a good idea to work out your own debts, instead of worrying about others."

His book opened by itself with an image of Tobias and Elijah lying dead in front of their grieving wives and small children.

Kenny stared at the open book in the middle of the table. The screams and cries went to his very core. He was not convinced that slavery was wrong, but he did think that he could have stopped this tragedy. He thought that old man Jensen had gone too far. He had never considered these men to be fathers or husbands. The longer he was forced to see wives and children crying over bloody corpses, the more his heart softened. Kenny remembered how he really felt, hiding in that ditch with his friends. He recalled the remorse and shame that he could not admit.

Tobias and Elijah stood silently next to the table as Kenny faced his past. Finally, he put his hands over his ears and closed his eyes. "Make it stop! Make it stop!" Kenny pleaded.

The book slammed shut in front of him and the screams and cries silenced. Kenny opened his eyes and looked at Tobias and Elijah.

"I ... I am so sorry for not stepping up to save you. I did not expect any of that to happen and was scared to let my friends know how I was really feeling. Please forgive me."

Tobias put his hand on Kenny's shoulder, as Elijah looked him in the eye. Potter interjected.

"It is forgiven."

Tobias and Elijah smiled tearfully as Potter continued.

"I grieve the hate that you have carried all these years."

Kenny was shaking as he looked up at them. Tobias and Elijah walked around the table to Potter and gave him a hug. They both told Kenny they hoped to be seeing him soon. They walked into the meadow where two horse-drawn carriages transported them across the meadow and out of sight.

"And that is how it is done," Potter said.

Kenny turned toward Potter.

"How come they forgave me so fast?" Kenny asked.

"When they got here, they were both filled with anger and hatred. They both realized that carrying around someone else's burden was not going to set them free. The truth was, it was old man Jensen, his farm hands, and you that had the burden to carry. Once they realized that, they were set free."

"How do you know so much about it? Were you their guide too?" Kenny asked.

Potter nodded his head as he slid the book back toward Kenny.

"You are doing well, so let's continue," Potter said.

Kenny bristled at the thought of Potter being in a position of authority over him.

"Listen, Potter, I will do this in my own time. Nobody, especially someone like you, is going to keep me from my heavenly reward!"

FOURTEEN

"YOU ARE the only hindrance to your heavenly reward, Kenny." Potter said.

Kenny wondered what Potter meant by that comment as he picked up his book of life. He read about his years in school and was surprised by the intimate detail of every page. He read about the day his brother Billy had an argument with his father in the barn. Kenny was coming home from school and thought he would go to the barn to pet the stray cat that lived there. As he approached, he heard yelling. Kenny stopped just outside to listen. He had never heard his brother talk to his father like this. Billy was now a young man of twenty and was standing up to his father for the first time in his life. He heard Billy yell at his father.

"Now that I know the secret, I cannot stay!"

He heard his father crying as Billy said he was heading north to find work, vowing never to return.

His big brother climbed on his horse and galloped out of the stables past Kenny. He remembered feeling heartsick watching his brother riding away from the estate.

"I never did understand that argument. I did not know there was a family secret," Kenny said.

Potter looked at Kenny compassionately. "What happened that day you ran to the gully?"

Kenny squirmed and frowned. "I already told you!"

"You have told me what you were told to remember," Potter patiently said.

Kenny was anxious and scared. He didn't want to look at this, but Potter continued probing.

"Tell me what happened, Kenny."

Filled with anger and fear, Kenny paused on that page, not wanting to turn to the next.

"The truth shall set you free," Potter assured him.

His words gave Kenny the resolve he needed. He started to remember more as he turned the page . . .

Little Kenny Wilson ran down the hill behind the mansion. The smell of honeysuckle filled the air. As he looked into the gully, he saw a mound of fresh dirt and his father laying down a shovel.

His father whipped around with fear in his eyes. He was shocked to see little Kenny standing above him.

"I have some bad news for you, son. I know you always thought your friendship with that little black boy was a secret, but it wasn't," he said.

Kenny slowly sat on the edge of the gully, trying to understand what his father was saying. He looked at the mound of dirt at his father's feet and wondered what was happening. The elder Jensen seemed to be scrambling for an explanation as he wiped his sweaty brow. He pointed toward the shantytown.

"Those people do not respect family and life like we do, son. If they think their kids will take food out of their mouths, they will just kill them so that they have more for themselves!"

Kenny screamed and cried out, "No, daddy, no!" He buried his face in his father's chest, sobbing uncontrollably.

His father whispered, "They have taken your friend. I'm sorry."

Kenny's sorrow turned to rage. He thought about Jeremiah, and wondered how his own parents could kill him just because they didn't want to feed him. He decided at that moment that Negroes were less than human.

Stunned, Kenny looked up from the pages. That memory had been sequestered for many years. He felt tremendous sadness for his friend Jeremiah, but could not get past the idea of what his parents had done. He banged his fist on the table and glared at Potter.

"This is why I thought none of you folks would be in heaven," Kenny said.

Potter shook his head. "I am so sorry you have been burdened by your father's lies all this time. It is a weight you should not have had to bear."

Kenny quickly stood from the table. "How dare you call my father a liar!"

Potter calmly said, "It is not your fault you believed your father. You were a vulnerable child. If only those around you could have been like the little children."

Kenny ran his fingers through his hair, pacing back and forth in front of the table. "Why do we have to look at this in order for me to receive my eternal rest?"

Potter leaned back in his chair and looked up into the sprawling oak tree overhead. A cardinal gazed down and chirped happily. Potter winked at the bird.

"You will have no rest without knowing why you were the way you were," Potter said.

A breeze turned the page and Kenny looked back at the book. He was relieved to see that Potter had apparently moved on. He walked back to the table and sat. At the top of the page was an image of his father, Sebastian Wilson. Sebastian was riding his horse through the night. He was headed for shanties that housed his many slaves. A golden campfire was set in the center of the camp. The slaves gathered there to talk and sing away their daily struggles. The singing and laughter stopped as Sebastian Wilson entered their encampment.

"I am looking for a housekeeper. Bring out the women in the camp," Sebastian ordered.

All the women in the camp were brought out and lined up in front of Sebastian Wilson. Sebastian dismounted and started taking a closer look. He stopped halfway down the line and looked into the eyes of a beautiful young woman.

"What is your name?" Sebastian asked.

"Her name is Allyson. She is my wife," said a young man standing behind her.

Sebastian looked up at him and yelled.

"I was not talking to you!" Sebastian grabbed her arm and said, "You are coming with me!"

Her husband stepped up, yelling and pleading.

Sebastian turned around and backhanded his face. He and the woman mounted the horse and rode out of the camp.

Kenny looked up from the page. "I remember Allyson. She was nice to me. I remember her playing with me in the house. She got pregnant and then she was sent back to her family."

Potter looked at Kenny as though waiting for something to sink in.

The next page was all about the night Kenny listened to his parents arguing in the parlor. He was tucked into bed when he started to hear their voices. He got out of bed and crept down the hall. He could hear his mother crying and yelling through the parlor door at the bottom of the grand staircase. The door opened and his mother stormed out into the foyer.

She spun around and wagged her finger in the air.

"Send that little tramp back where she belongs!"

Sebastian hurried past her and found Allyson in the kitchen. She was ordered out of the house immediately.

Allyson gave birth to a baby boy five months later. He was named Jeremiah, after his grandfather. As he grew, he became friends with little Kenny Wilson. They would meet in the gully between their two worlds. There was an uncommon bond between the two boys. One morning Mrs. Wilson was in her flower garden picking roses. She heard rustling in the bushes down below her. She looked down the hill and saw Kenny and Jeremiah laughing and giggling as they rolled down the hill together. She threw down her pruning shears and headed straight for the house. She marched into her husband's office and slammed the door. The book-lined oak walls reverberated as Sebastian looked up from his papers.

"That little bastard is now becoming friends with our Kenny. This must stop! Get rid of them all before your sin catches up with us!"

That night there was a raid on the shanty camp. People ran in all directions as the horsemen ran through the camp. They announced that there was property stolen from the Wilsons. All the shanties were ransacked. Allyson and her husband were pulled out of the camp after they were accused of having silver forks in their possession. Allyson screamed as her four-year-old boy was taken from her arms. The parents were dragged one way, and young Jeremiah was handed over to Sebastian. The horses raced out of the camp in two different directions.

As the morning came, a fresh mound of earth was piled in a gully behind the Wilson mansion. The sun tried hard to bring light to the truth that had been buried there. Two young slaves, a man and a woman were sold at auction never to be seen again.

Kenny put down the book. He looked up with tears in his eyes. Potter was crying, too.

"The sins of the father will visit many generations. This lie has defined you," Potter said.

Kenny was trying to take in the awful truth. Everything he had been told, everything he thought he knew, was gone. His eyes widened, and his face contorted. He was about to scream when a warm light embraced him. His horror and pain were instantly blunted by pure, unconditional love. He could feel the ugly truth of his childhood being bathed in acceptance and grace. The light seemed to understand. Kenny felt his angst being carried away by the warmth surrounding him.

Potter welcomed the light tending Kenny's needs. The two men basked in the glow of its boundless love. A mighty gust rushed over the meadow heading straight toward the oak tree. The wind crashed into the light, creating a whooshing vacuum. Kenny looked around him. All the trees and flowers were bending and twisting, yet his book of life lay strangely still on the table. The wind was harnessed by the light, and with it, his burden was lifted. The knowledge of the past was there, but the pain had been carried away. Kenny watched the brightness subside as leaves fell from the mighty oak tree.

FIFTEEN

KENNY SAT DUMFOUNDED by what had just happened.

"The comforter could not allow you to receive that news without his help," Potter said, gazing across the meadow.

Kenny shifted in his chair. "The hatred is gone. I felt it die in the light."

Potter looked at him from across the table. "Now you understand where the hatred came from."

Kenny nodded his head in silent affirmation.

Potter stood. "Let's take a walk."

Kenny nodded and slowly stood.

Potter pointed at the table. "You'd better bring your book."

Kenny placed it in his pocket. He had been given new clothes, the clothes of a humble farmer. The light blue shirt fit well. Suspenders held up the brown pants that were tucked into tall brown boots. Kenny had always prided himself on his dress and was particularly fond of his Confederate uniform.

Clearly sensing Kenny's unease, Potter said, "There are no uniforms here, just the whole armor of God and the breastplate of His righteousness."

Kenny followed Potter across the meadow. He stopped abruptly when he spotted a skunk waddling toward them. Potter laughed and knelt to pet his head. The skunk rubbed his face against Potter's hand. He rose with a smile, and they continued toward the trees.

"It seems like you are looking at all this beauty for the first time. If you are a guide around here, haven't you seen all of this before?" Kenny asked.

"Creation is always expanding. With each increase comes new life. I never grow tired of proclaiming, 'It is good!' Many plans were drawn and input given before your arrival. It is just good to see all the hard work really paid off," Potter said.

"Were you in on all the decisions for this place?" Kenny asked.

Potter chuckled. "I was honored to be a part of it."

They came to a covered wooden bridge that crossed a quiet stream. It was painted red with white trim. As they entered, their footsteps echoed. An owl blinked at them from the rafters as they passed beneath his watchful eye.

Kenny recalled an encounter with the enemy on a covered bridge during the war. He had been separated from his unit and was heading across country in a rainstorm. Cold and exhausted, he saw a covered bridge and ran toward it for shelter. He remembered sitting down against the wall to rest and get dry. Hearing horses approaching, he scrambled to his feet. Slinging his rifle over his shoulder, Kenny crawled up the inside of the covered bridge.

The two Union soldiers were wounded. Apparently, they too thought the bridge would be a good place to rest. Kenny straddled a crossbeam high above them and watched them dismount from their horses. Both Union soldiers appeared to have lost a lot of blood. They leaned against the wall and tended to their wounds.

Noticing the soldiers' packs brimming with food and supplies, Kenny's stomach growled and his survival instinct took hold. He slowly crept down to the bridge floor. The horses stirred as he crouched behind them. When the soldiers nodded off, he rummaged through their supplies.

Potter watched Kenny as he looked up into the rafters and all around the covered bridge.

"I was on a bridge like this during the war," Kenny said.

"Oh?" said Potter.

"Yeah, I ran into some Yanks and stole their food to survive," Kenny said.

Potter looked at him and asked, "Is that all you stole from them?"

"Hey, listen, it was war. I had to do what was necessary to survive."

Potter shook his head. "I am not talking about the beef jerky, apples, and water. Let's take a look at what your book has recorded."

Kenny frowned and stepped back. "You were not there. War is hell!"

The book opened in his hand. Kenny looked down at an image of a covered bridge in a rainstorm . . .

The apples and jerky were giving him strength. Kenny kept a suspicious eye on the sleeping soldiers. He gulped down water from a canteen and looked with disdain at the wounded men. The idea that they could dare defend the freedom of slaves galled him. There was no defense for taking sides with those godless heathens. The more he thought about it, the angrier he became. He slowly slid his rifle off his shoulder and took aim at the head of the nearest man. The bullet hit his temple, killing him instantly. The second man awakened and Kenny shoved a knife deep into his chest. By all accounts, a Confederate soldier murdered two wounded Union soldiers merely seeking refuge from a storm . . .

"Bradley Mason and Anthony Barnes were their names. You took their lives because of your blind hatred. This was not self-defense. This was murder," Potter said.

Kenny immediately felt the shame and remorse that he had buried in anger. With his long-held justification for the crime now gone, all that remained was the memory of two helpless men being slaughtered, by him, and in cold blood.

"What have I done?" Kenny said, dropping to his knees. "I killed two innocent men. God forgive me."

His book fell from his hands and opened on the floor of the bridge. Just as he begged for forgiveness, the images and words on the page vanished.

He picked the book up and stared at the blank pages. He looked up at Potter. "How did that happen?"

"You asked for forgiveness, so the record was wiped clean," Potter said.

Kenny got to his feet with his book clutched in his hand. He looked around. "Is God listening to us?"

"He is always with you," Potter answered.

Potter turned and headed across the covered bridge with Kenny at his side.

They walked down a dirt road with a fence holding back a thick forest. On the right was a cotton field. Strolling in silence, Kenny was drawn to the white fields. They reminded him of home.

Potter asked, "What are you thinking about?"

Kenny stopped in the middle of the road with a smile on his face. "These fields remind me of home. I remember, fondly, the sounds of the spirituals being sung from the fields of our plantation."

Potter grimaced. "Is that the way you remember it?"

Kenny nodded, still smiling. Potter snatched the book from his hand and marched straight into the cotton fields. Kenny followed. They reached a spot in the midst of the field.

Potter opened the book, showing it to Kenny. He looked down at the image on the page, and Potter touched it with his hand. All around them slaves picked cotton in the blistering sun. The slaves were tired and hungry, and their fingers bled from the thistles. A white man on horseback rode through the fields barking orders. As the rider approached, he rode right through Kenny and Potter. Kenny saw that the rider was himself, lording over the exhausted men and women. He stopped his horse in front of two older slaves that were withering in the sun. "You're going too slowly! You're costing my family money!"

He pulled out his whip and began beating the two older men. When he was finished, he yelled, "Let that be a lesson to the rest of you!"

Potter gazed at Kenny. "Wealth was made on the backs of free slave labor. Do you have any idea how much money all those workers made your family?"

"It was just business. These slaves were property of the Wilson plantation. As I grew, I was responsible for profits. I was given a bonus from my father based on how much production I could get out of the slaves. It was the only way to do business." Kenny explained.

"Well, there must have been some people who thought there was another way, because they had a Civil War over the issue," Potter said.

Suddenly, Kenny's back began to sting. His hands cramped, and his fingers began bleeding. His knees ached, and his body became drenched in sweat. All around him, the workers stood up in the fields to stare at him.

The cotton fields turned to gold coins, hip deep in all directions. The workers' faces grew somber as they glared at their former owner. The coin level began to rise as blood bubbled up through the gold pieces. All the slaves stood on top of the sea of blood and gold, and Kenny suddenly felt himself drowning. When a gold coin lodged in his windpipe, he splashed and thrashed, trying to breathe. He went under.

Two strong hands grabbed him. He looked at his rescuers. They were the two he had whipped in the field. They stood atop the gold and blood. Kenny spat and coughed, and the coin dislodged from his throat.

"Please forgive me," he gasped.

Potter closed the book, and they were once again on the road overlooking the pristine white fields of cotton.

"*I have come to set the captives free,*" Potter said.

Kenny looked at him with eyes wide open. "All those faces, all those people I terrorized in slavery. I never thought their lives were significant."

"*You* are the captive I am referring to," Potter said.

Potter's words hit a place deep inside his spirit. Kenny could not shake the images he had just experienced. It gave him a perspective he could never have imagined. The pampered lifestyle he had been afforded was a direct result of hundreds of slaves. But it was he who was the one enslaved in a mindset of entitlement.

Potter handed him his book. Kenny quickly leafed through the pages looking for incidents where he had directly or indirectly enslaved others for personal gain. All references to his involvement in slavery had been erased.

He looked up from the book and saw Potter smiling.

"Anyone who asks for forgiveness will be given it. This is all a part of your journey to find the Father."

Relief flooded Kenny's senses. They walked side by side. Potter had Kenny account for more incidents in his book. He still had to answer for the times he had stolen and cheated others. Kenny wanted to know how Billy had found the family secret regarding his father and Jeremiah. Potter opened the book.

Every spring the rains had threatened flooding of the plantation. Sebastian Wilson had given Billy the task of coming up with a solution to this problem. Billy spent weeks surveying the property. Riding from the nearby lake to the far corners of their property, he thought if he could harness the flow of the water, they could minimize the damage. He rode along the gully that ran through the property between the shanties and the rest of the estate. His plan consisted of digging a series of trenches from the gully to disperse the water flow. The ravine and two other large trenches would eventually spill downhill into a lake at the west end of their property. He was proud of his idea and told his father he had solved the problem. His father had questions, but Billy assured him he could trust him. Sebastian

Wilson saw his son's eagerness to impress him and decided to trust his judgment.

Billy took the plans off his father's desk.

"I will make you proud, Father."

He ran from his dad's office ready to begin this large project.

SIXTEEN

BILLY HAD ASKED for fifty slaves to complete the project. Sebastian granted his request. Sebastian decided to take a vacation with his wife before the spring rains came. He put Billy in charge of his younger siblings while they were gone. Billy assured his father that his plan would be complete before his return.

Trenches were being dug by early the next morning. Billy was riding up and down the property, seeing the beginnings of his plan taking shape. Day and night he had the slaves digging.

One morning, a week into his project, he was riding along the gully behind the mansion. Slaves were digging two trenches out from the gully. A roar of screams rang up from the crowd as they gathered around the hole they had dug. Billy heard the commotion and rode quickly up to see what was happening.

He dismounted his horse, looking down into the gully.

"Hey, why aren't you digging?" he barked.

The men grumbled. He stepped down into the gully and through the crowd. The crowd parted, and Billy looked down into the dirt. A small skeleton wrapped in a blanket lay at the bottom of the hole.

Billy crouched to get a closer look. He brushed back the dirt. He immediately recognized the blanket. It was a horse blanket especially made for Sebastian Wilson. He remembered that his mother had these monogrammed blankets made for her husband on Christmas eleven years earlier. Clutched in the small skeletal hand was a cameo pendant that had sprung open. The image of Sebastian Wilson stared up at the crowd.

The night the shantytown had been raided, Allyson seemed to know why they were there. She had stolen a cameo from the mansion as a sort of insurance. When the horses rode in, she took the cameo from her skirt pocket along with a small paring knife she had pilfered from the mansion. Allyson quickly opened the cameo and scratched something on the inside. She clamped it shut and gave it to Jeremiah. "Whatever happens, do not open your hand," she said.

Billy picked up the cameo. He could feel the eyes of the crowd staring at him. His hand began to shake as he stared at his father's picture and the scrawled letters A-L-L-Y.

Billy remembered a day when he was in his father's study. Allyson was dusting as Billy sat doing his homework. Billy and Allyson began to talk about reading and writing. Billy spent that afternoon teaching his housemaid "Ally", as they called her, how to spell her nickname.

He stood and gave the command, "Digging is over! Go back to camp!" He pushed his way through the crowd and scrambled out of the gully. He mounted his horse and rode off toward the house.

Sebastian Wilson returned to the property. When his carriage drove toward the house he noticed unfinished trenches with shovels lying scattered nearby. He informed his wife that he had to check the progress of Billy's project and hurried toward the gully in back of the mansion. Instantly, he saw the hole with his dirty monogrammed horse blanket. He rushed into the barn calling out Billy's name. Billy came out from a horse stall, glaring at his father, and threw the cameo in his father's face.

Kenny said. "That's where I came strolling up to pet the stray cat in the barn."

"Exactly," said Potter.

"How did Billy end up in the Union army?" Kenny asked.

Potter walked beside him on the dirt road. "Billy rode north to find work. The tensions in the country over slavery becoming more heated coincided with the division he had experienced in your family. He got a job on a large ranch. He worked hard to forget the horror of his past by becoming an asset to his employer. His knowledge of horses gave him an opportunity to become a horse trainer and buyer. When the war broke out, the army needed horses. Billy became a buyer for the Union army. He wanted to do more, and after six months in the procurement department, he transferred to the cavalry. He charged through the woods toward the Shiloh church after his horse was shot out from under him. A bullet entered his chest, and he collapsed thirty feet from the church's front steps."

"I didn't know that was him!" Kenny cried.

Potter put his arm around him and said, "I know."

They walked in silence. The bright sky brought new colors to the flowers and trees. Lions and sheep were grazing in the same fields. The scene brought him joy.

Potter gazed at the pastoral scene. "It is very good." He said.

They continued talking about other incidents in Kenny's life while paging through the accounts, praising the good and erasing the bad. Kenny's burden was becoming lighter with each page. Each step brought new life and new hope in his soul. He had become very attached to his guide and friend, Potter. He wanted Potter to show him how to get to the Father. The further they walked, the more anxious he became to be in His presence.

Potter stopped and pointed down the road. Kenny saw a bright golden city shining in a distant valley.

"We are almost there!" Potter cheered.

They hugged one another, and Potter took off running toward the city. Kenny laughed and chased after his friend. The faster they ran, the more energy he received. The trees and flowers were becoming a blur as they raced down the road.

Suddenly, Potter stopped and laughed; Kenny ran into him.

"There seems to be a welcoming committee," Potter said.

Kenny looked down the road. The golden light of the city silhouetted two figures on the road. Kenny shaded his eyes to see one tall and one short figure on the road to the Holy City.

Kenny walked past Potter slowly. His eyes shimmered with tears. Billy and Jeremiah rushed toward their brother. The three hugged and danced as they relished in one another's company.

"Who arranged this?" Kenny asked.

Billy and Jeremiah pointed over Kenny's shoulder.

Kenny turned around to see his young black guide standing in a pillar of bright light. Potter's face changed a thousand times in seconds. Black to brown, woman to man, Chinese to Indian. Shards of light shot from his head and far into the sky above. The ground trembled as He began to speak.

"I am the potter and you are the clay."

All three Wilson boys fell to their knees. Kenny looked into the face of a young handsome man with olive skin and black wavy hair. His cropped black beard framed his perfect smiling face. Kenny realized to whom he had talked all this time and began to shudder. He fell on his face at His feet. Helped up by Billy and Jeremiah, he pleaded for forgiveness.

The Potter hugged Kenny tight. "I forgive you, my precious one."

Kenny thought about the name Potter, and how he had come to him in the form of one whom he had hated most.

Kenny laughed at the irony. "I wasn't very pliable clay!"

This brought a big laugh from all of them as little Jeremiah climbed up on the Potter's shoulders.

Billy's love for horses was exemplified as he presented a white horse to Kenny.

"He has given me the honor of taking care of His horse, and getting him ready for your arrival," Billy said.

Kenny stroked the mane of the beautiful stallion.

"Regal, this is Kenny," the Potter said.

Kenny was handed a royal robe of purple, and he mounted the horse. Jeremiah climbed off the Potter's shoulders to help Billy lead the horse toward the gate.

The archangel Gabriel appeared on the top of the archway overlooking the gate. A beautiful trumpet blast announced Kenny's arrival. Peter opened the gate, and the white horse was led under the archway. A thunderous roar went up from the crowd. A choir broke into a triumphant song, especially written for Kenny. After the choir completed its song, Kenny noticed that Billy joined other men lining both sides of the street paved in gold. Gabriel brought his trumpet to his lips. The men saluted when they heard 'Taps' being played.

Potter looked at Kenny and said, "We just paid tribute to all those who died at Shiloh. The men lining the streets are the soldiers who died that day."

A banquet was set in an enormous marble structure called the Hall of Eternity. As Kenny arrived in front of the hall, royal purple carpet was rolled out and down the stairs. Huge crowds gathered on both sides as they ascended the stairs. When they reached the top, Potter turned him around to face the immense crowd.

"This is Kenneth Jordan Wilson. He was a lost sheep, straying in the wilderness of prejudice and hatred. He has returned to the fold."

The throng burst into cheers. The two of them waved at the crowd. Kenny cried tears of joy.

They turned to enter the hall.

"We usually invite everyone to these banquets, but I thought it might be interesting to just have a meal with four hundred of your new friends," Potter said.

Kenny's eyes grew wide as the massive doors opened. They walked into a cavernous hall with marble floors and huge pillars surrounding a common area. In front of them was a series of banquet tables.

Billy and Jeremiah walked in behind them. Kenny looked at his guests. At each table sat all the former slaves that had died over the years on the Wilson plantation, faces he knew from childhood.

The two older men that he abused in the cotton fields walked toward them.

One said, "Welcome, we are glad you are here."

Billy and Jeremiah sat at the head table as Kenny and the Potter walked through the room.

When they arrived at the front of the vast hall, the Potter turned to Kenny. "We are going to serve these fine guests that have agreed to have dinner with you," He said enthusiastically.

He slapped Kenny on the back and told him to follow Him to the kitchen. They picked up trays filled with prepared plates of food and headed back into the hall. Each guest was served before Kenny and the Potter sat to share the meal.

As Kenny ate, guests would come by his table and say "Hi" or welcome him home. He got a chance to talk at length with his brothers, Billy and Jeremiah. He asked for forgiveness for Shiloh.

Billy smiled. "You never were that good a shot when we used to hunt squirrels."

Kenny asked Jeremiah why he had not grown. He replied that Mama Allyson wanted to raise him by herself from that day they became separated. He explained that he arrived home first and waited for her. She said that getting over the hatred and resentment was a long process for her.

Just then, Mama Allyson walked toward the table. Kenny asked for her forgiveness on behalf of his family.

She said, "It took me a while, but I realized that what happened was Sebastian Wilson's burden, not mine. Jeremiah forgave as a little child, but I was not so willing."

The Potter reached across the table and took her hand in His.

"Everyone has their own path. I am so blessed that you are here."

Allyson thanked Him. She faced Kenny. "I tried to get Jeremiah to sit at my table, but he just had to sit with his brothers."

They all laughed. Kenny put his arms around Billy and Jeremiah.

After the festive meal, Kenny stood at the front doors of the Hall of Eternity thanking each guest as they left. A sense of family, beyond any human understanding, filled Kenny's spirit. The Potter and Kenny cleaned the vast hall, washing all the dishes, pots, and pans. Kenny mopped the floors and put away hundreds of tables and chairs. A quiet sense of accomplishment swept over him as he looked across the empty hall.

"Are you ready to see your new home?" the Potter asked.

Kenny nodded his head. In the twinkling of an eye, they were standing behind a mansion with large barns and clover fields where horses stood grazing. They walked toward the architectural master-piece, and Kenny took it all in. As they neared the main house, they took a right on a flagstone walk. Past the pristine barns was a two-story farmhouse with a small front porch. Vibrant flowers framed the walkway. Kenny looked back at the mansion and pointed. "Isn't that my house?"

"No, that is the home of Tobias. He and his friend Elijah have adjoining estates. I asked them to take you on as a ranch hand. They have built you this farmhouse as a welcoming gift. You will start by caring for of all the animals on both properties. You will be given greater challenges and opportunities as you grow in grace and knowl-edge," the Potter said.

Kenny looked back at his farmhouse and smiled. It was a beauti-fully simple home, built with love. He felt a deep sense of gratitude that he had been shown such grace.

He walked around the back of the home and Potter followed. In the meadow was an oak tree with a table and chairs underneath the canopy of leaves.

"My destiny was that close, and I didn't see it," Kenny said.

They sat at the table under the leafy canopy. His book with a compass insignia on the cover lay closed on the table. Kenny picked it up and ran his hands across the cover.

"It really did give me the direction I needed," he said.

He looked up at the Potter, whose smile conveyed a deep sense of pride.

"Well done, Kenny. I am so proud to have helped you on your journey home."

"When will I see you again? What If I have questions?" Kenny asked.

The Potter smiled, and said, "I will never leave you or forsake you. Whenever you want to talk, I promise to meet you here under your oak tree."

He stood and Kenny rose to hug him. The birds chirped in the tree above them.

The Potter smiled then dissolved into bright light and soared high above the oak tree. A gentle wind brushed Kenny's face.

A resounding voice echoed through the hills and valleys. *"This is the Word that came to Kenneth from the Lord. Go down to the Potter's house and there, I will give you my message."*

SEVENTEEN

THE SUPERSTAR

"For all that is in the world--the desire of the flesh, the desire of the
eyes, the pride in riches--comes not from the Father..."
1 John 2:16

HE HEARD the fans chanting for an encore as he made his way back
stage. Security guards escorted him through the hallways of the
arena. A crowd had already formed around his tour bus as he climbed
aboard. The bus pulled through the giant loading doors. He looked
out the window, smiling at the enormous sign on the side of the arena.
It read, "Bobby Lane in Concert." It never ceased to amaze him.
Bobby couldn't believe thousands of people were still flocking to his
shows.

Bobby got a drink from his fully stocked bar and made his way to
the back of the bus to retrieve his pills. He sank into the plush leather
couch and watched the sleet and snow pelting the windows.

Bobby leaned forward to the driver. "What is the weather
supposed to do? Get better or worse?"

"It's going to get worse before we're through," the driver said.

"I have to be in Indianapolis by tomorrow night. Make it happen!" Bobby yelled.

"Yes, sir, Mr. Lane," the driver said.

A small fleet of trucks had already arrived in Indianapolis in advance of his next concert. Hundreds of lighting and sound technicians, and staging and set designers, were employed for each tour.

Bobby lay down on the couch and tried to rest.

The superstar had been asleep for several hours when a sharp jolt awakened him. Items were flying off the shelves. He bolted up. The bus began swerving from left to right. He stumbled toward the front.

"Are you trying to kill us?" he screamed.

The driver was too busy to respond. The luxury coach had hit a patch of ice on a high mountain bridge, and they were skidding sideways. Bobby glanced out the side window. A jack-knifed tractor-trailer was hurling towards them.

Shattering glass and crunching metal drowned out their screams. Both vehicles ripped through the guardrail, tumbling downward through the cold winter night.

Bobby opened his mouth, prepared to scream. A beautiful melody filled his throat. He opened his eyes to see a flock of cardinals joining him in song. He was lying on his back under a sprawling oak tree. He closed his mouth. The birds continued to chirp and flutter. Slowly, he pulled himself to a sitting position and leaned against the trunk of the tree. The beautiful melody that had replaced his screams made him think perhaps he was delusional. Bobby was sure he had suffered a severe concussion. Cautiously he reached behind his head, expecting to find a bloody mess. There was no wound. He did not even have a headache.

He remembered the blurring flashes of his life as he plummeted toward the bottom of the ravine. The snowy rocks awaited him below. The horror of his reality had made him scream as he closed his eyes for impact. That memory contradicted everything he was now seeing. He patted himself, finding no broken bones or injuries. He noticed his stage clothes had been replaced. He was now wearing a pair of faded blue jeans, a black t-shirt, and black boots. He didn't recall changing clothes after the show. There had been many times over the years that he had changed out of his stage clothes and disappeared after a show. He would rent, buy, or steal a luxury sports car, get drunk, and race through the city. This pattern would sometimes result in accidents. His army of lawyers and handlers would always clean up the aftermath. But this . . . he looked around. *This* defied explanation. There was no evidence of a wreck.

A sense of calm confusion filled his spirit. *Maybe I just dodged another bullet.*

Bobby stood and took in the surroundings. The overhanging branches of the oak tree swayed in a light breeze. The lone tree was in the middle of a meadow on the floor of a deep canyon. Waterfalls fell in various places out of steep moss-covered rocks. The meadow was surrounded on three sides by canyon walls. The fourth side was a sloping hill filled with wildflowers. Bobby began walking toward the slope.

When he reached the canyon rim, he looked back. He was astonished at how far he had traveled. It seemed to have only taken a few minutes to climb to the top. He noticed the more energy he exerted, the more he received. Bobby knew he should be exhausted, and yet he had never felt better.

The oak tree and meadow appeared very small in the distance. The mist from the various waterfalls created a double rainbow. Light shimmered on a placid lake on the canyon floor.

Bobby turned around to see a paved road in front of him. At his feet was a guitar case. He knelt and opened it. The entertainer's eyes grew wide as he recognized his first guitar lying in the case. He ran his fingers across the strings. He smiled. The sight of a silent, white bus cresting the hill interrupted his thoughts. Bobby closed the case and picked it up. He stuck out his thumb and the bus slowed to stop. Bobby looked at the destination panel on the front of the bus. It read, "Homeward Bound."

The doors opened. Bobby had had many drivers over the years.

Most of them he never bothered to notice. They were just there to transport him to the next gig. But this driver got his attention. A smiling boy sat in the driver's seat. His uniform consisted of a starched white shirt, black necktie, and black pants. His dark wavy hair crowned his olive-skinned face.

"Do you need a ride?" the boy asked. His piercing eyes and friendly presence unnerved Bobby.

"I seem to be lost. Can you help me?" Bobby asked.

"This is the way walk you in it." said the smiling driver.

The boy appeared no more than twelve. Bobby eyed him with suspicion. "How old are you?" he asked.

The boy sat up straight in the driver's seat. He grabbed the wheel with both hands. "Older than you might think."

"Did my manager arrange for you to pick me up?" Bobby asked.

"No, my father told me to come and get you," he said.

"How is it that a small boy is able to drive a bus? I mean, what if we get stopped by the authorities?"

The young driver smiled proudly. "Around here, my father is the ultimate authority."

Bobby was still confused but desperate enough to board the tour bus. There had been several times in the course of a national tour that his bus would break down. When that occurred, his management team would arrange for another bus to pick him up. He noticed that the inside of this bus was an exact replica of his custom coach. Bobby set the guitar case down and took a seat on the plush leather couch. He did not believe the boy. He knew his manager must have arranged this. Maybe this was payback for all the trouble he had caused. The bus doors closed as they pulled out on the open road.

He sat back. Shivers went up his spine as he recalled the accident. He couldn't imagine how he had survived that horrific crash.

Bobby leaned forward to the young driver. "Did you hear about an accident on a bridge last night?"

"There are no accidents here. Everything is as it is meant to be," the boy said, with an authority that belied his age.

Frustrated, Bobby asked, "What is your name, and who do you work for?"

The boy smiled. "I am about my father's business. My name is Sonny Elway."

"Why does your daddy think it okay to have a boy drive this big bus?" Bobby asked.

"He has faith in me," Sonny said. "I have been given the opportunity to take you where you need to go."

"I told you I was lost," Bobby said.

Sonny nodded. "I know. My father thought that a little child should lead you."

The international musical icon became furious. He was used to being in charge. He had a staff of dozens who took care of his every need. He stood and walked to his bar. There was no liquor, only spring water and several kinds of fruit juice.

Bobby called out, "My manager has specific instructions when we get a replacement bus. Everything is spelled out in my rider. This is not what I asked for!"

Sonny said, "We are not willing to give you everything you asked for."

Bobby exhaled in exasperation as he headed for the bedroom at the back of the bus. He knelt beside the bed and pulled the drawer out from the nightstand. He flipped it over, expecting to find a plastic bag taped to the bottom. His manager always took care of supplying his drugs. It was one of his many unspoken duties. Bobby found no pills. As he replaced the drawer, he realized he no longer craved the drugs or alcohol. He made his way back to the front of the bus. He took a seat in the booth on the right side of the bus. From there he could see his young driver. In front of him on the table was a tattered tour book. The cover read, "Bobby Lane: The Final Tour." He was used to seeing tour books but never bothered to read them. They contained all the contact information, lists of venues, and dates and times of the current tour. He relied on his manager to tell him where he was going. He sighed, shaking his head.

"Is there something wrong?" Sonny asked, looking in the rearview mirror.

Bobby looked out the window as the bus wound its way past a small town nestled in a green valley. Often asleep while on the bus, going from gig to gig, he had missed so much beauty while he was on the road.

"Wrong?" Bobby asked. "Is there anything wrong? Yeah, I'd say there is a lot wrong. A *kid* is driving me around and nothing in my bus is where I expect it to be." He picked up the tour book. "Even the tour book is wrong. This tour is supposed to be named after my latest album. This book has the wrong title on it."

"Are you kidding?" Sonny asked.

"It says 'Bobby Lane: The Final Tour' on the cover. I have complete creative control over my tour. If there had been a tour name-change, I would have had to sign off on it."

"You signed off on it when you asked for help," Sonny said.

"What do you mean?" Bobby asked the boy.

"Well, when you were falling toward the floor of that rocky ravine, you cried out for God's help."

"Wait. I thought you said you didn't know about an accident on the bridge!"

The young man piped up, "No, no, what I said was there are no accidents here. Time and chance happen to all people. Your accident happened back there, not here."

Bobby rubbed his whiskered chin. "Just how far have we come?"

"As far as east is from the west," Sonny answered.

"If you heard me cry for help, then you must have been there. Why didn't you go get some help?"

Sonny looked over his shoulder. "Do you remember splintering against the rocks?"

Bobby shook his head

"The moment you cried for help, the fear of death mercifully answered," the boy explained.

"Did you say *death*?" Bobby asked.

"Well, death to that existence, anyway."

"You are not making any sense!" Bobby shouted.

"It is all explained right there in your tour book," Sonny said.

Bobby flicked his wrist. "I don't read those things. That's what managers are for."

"The answers you seek are in its pages," Sonny said. "I am here to take you through your book as we embark on this journey together."

EIGHTEEN

BOBBY OPENED the dog-eared tour book. He was surprised to find biographical information about his early life. It was an intricately detailed account. Robert Carl Langston was born to Maureen and Carl Langston. It had been a hard pregnancy. The Langstons were informed that the baby might not survive the night. Maureen was devastated. But Carl was hoping the doctors were right. He couldn't afford to feed another.

Robert was taken home to a three-room shack that sat adjacent to the railroad tracks. His first bed was a shabby plaid couch that sat in the largest room of their home. Cold winds and loud trains rattled the thin walls day and night. Maureen tried her best to shelter young Robert from the harsh reality that surrounded them. Poverty covered the Langstons like a wet blanket. Carl had given up. He wrapped himself in self-pity and anger. His only escape was drunkenness.

Maureen cleaned houses, took in ironing, and planted her own garden to keep the family fed. Robert grew up knowing his mother loved him but that his father thought he was a burden. Bobby once overheard his father telling his mother that 'the brat was costing too much'.

Robert was a gifted child. The constant rumbling of the train was annoying to most people. But it was a soundtrack to Robert. As a boy, he would sit on the front porch of their home, drumming his hands against his legs as the train roared by. He found different rhythms with different trains. Perhaps it was the promise of distant places that drew Robert. The monotonous rumblings became a part of him.

"You are the only one that could hear music from such noise," his mother would say.

"The song is different every day, Momma. You just have to listen." Robert would spend hours on the front steps, smiling at the passing locomotive.

"The trains became a part of your unique musical sound," Sonny said.

Bobby looked up from the tour book. "How did you know what I was reading?" Bobby asked.

"I know everything about you, Robert," Sonny said cheerfully.

"Are you some sort of crazed fan that has become obsessed with the idea of getting close to a celebrity?" Bobby asked.

The young boy laughed. "I will admit I have had you on my mind for as long as I can remember."

Bobby couldn't explain how this boy knew so much about him.

"Take a look at the last page. It was written seconds before you arrived here," Sonny said.

Bobby leafed to the final page. He read a detailed account of the concert. He read about being escorted to his bus. The book detailed the retrieval of his pills and whiskey. It recounted the conversation with the driver. The next section stunned him. It read, *"After 2.13 hours, encountered ice on a bridge stretching over a deep ravine. The tour bus collided with a semi-trailer. The impact caused both vehicles to crash through the guardrail. Falling through the air, Robert Carl Langston feared his impending demise. He cried out for help. Fright overwhelmed him. He was transformed from the physical realm."* This entry was followed by a series of mathematical equations and formulas.

"'Transformed from the physical realm'?--What does that mean?" Bobby asked.

"It means you have been given the chance at eternal life."

"Okay, that's it!" Bobby climbed out of the booth. "Stop the bus right now!"

Sonny slammed on the brakes.

He looked at the young driver on his way to the door. "I will find my own ride," Bobby said.

Sonny opened the bus doors. "I will be here. *I will never leave you or forsake you.*"

Bobby grumbled, stomped down the three steps, and exited the doors.

As soon as his feet touched the ground, everything around him dimmed. He was standing on an icy bridge. Hundreds of flickering candles glowed in the cold night air. He walked toward a crowd of people huddled in the middle of the bridge. Cars were lined up for miles along the side of the road. People walked across the bridge holding candles. Bobby noticed that no one seemed to recognize him. As though he were invisible, people looked right through him on their way to a makeshift shrine. On the left side of the bridge he saw a twisted metal guardrail ripped open, with sawhorses and orange cones forming a temporary barrier. Next to the gaping hole leaned a large cardboard poster of Bobby Lane. At the bottom of the poster were dozens of flowers and candles. Bobby gasped and slowly backed away from the scene and melted into the crowd, then retreated to the bus.

He banged on the doors. "Let me in!" Bobby pleaded.

The bus doors opened. He scrambled aboard, took a seat, and looked out the window. The vigil on the bridge had vanished and was replaced with rolling green valleys.

He called to the boy, "There was a ... a shrine. People were mourning me out there."

Sonny closed the doors and pulled back onto the road.

"It looked so . . . so *real*," Bobby whispered.

"It looked real because it was real. What you saw on the bridge was an attempt on their part to keep your memory alive. You know it's true. Just let it embrace you. You felt that you were no longer a part of that space or time," the young driver said.

Bobby flipped again to the back of the tour book to reread the last page. He looked up slowly with his eyes wide open. Realization was setting in.

"I didn't survive the fall," Bobby muttered.

"That is not entirely accurate. The fact is, all that makes you Robert survived. The physical shell that encased you shattered against those rocks," the boy explained.

Bobby stared out the window. He took in the magnificent beauty whisking by the window.

"I can't believe this is happening to me. This can't be the end."

"The end? The end is just the beginning!" Sonny said, with youthful enthusiasm.

Perception enveloped him. Life as he knew it was over.

Bobby snorted with defiance. "I long since gave up on the idea of an afterlife. The prospect of sitting around on clouds, singing praises at the feet of some God sounds ridiculous."

"I agree!" Sonny chuckled. "The eternal praises to the Father are made through the happiness and fulfillment of his children. Those praises are music to His ears. As far as the clouds go, we could cook up some fog on the road if that would make you feel better."

"This is not what I expected," Bobby said.

"The Father finds you wherever you are. He knows everything about you. He knows where you were at the moment of your transformation. The process is different for everyone. This is the road He has created especially for you."

Bobby listened, as he tried to understand his current state of being. "Well, obviously, there is life or some other dimension of existence after death, or I wouldn't be sitting here."

"Obviously," Sonny said, continuing to steer the luxury coach.

"I haven't believed in a heavenly Father since I was a boy. The whole idea of a God sitting on a throne writing down all my sins seems silly," said Bobby.

"When you put it that way, it sounds silly to me too," Sonny said.

"That's what they told me in church," Bobby explained.

"Maybe it's just what you heard, rather than what they taught," Sonny said.

"Do you believe all that stuff they tell you in church, Sonny?"

"All that stuff they tell you in church was translated through the prism of human understanding. Religion and spirituality are two very different things," Sonny explained.

Bobby listened to this boy who seemed wise beyond his years. "So, it's all fairy tales. I knew it!"

The boy laughed, "You just hear what you want to hear, don't you?"

Bobby didn't like this boy challenging him.

Sonny said, "The churches get a lot wrong, but they get a lot right, as well."

"I quit believing there was a God about the same time I figured out there was no Santa Claus," Bobby said.

Sonny gasped and his eyes grew wide. "Wait! There is no Santa Claus?"

Bobby scowled.

The young driver laughed out loud.

The silent bus made its way through a steep mountain pass. Sonny asked Bobby to reopen his tour book.

Tall white birch trees passed outside the window. With a heavy sigh, Bobby reluctantly obliged the boy's request.

Robert's mother insisted her boy go to church. The First Church of the Gospel was six blocks away. Maureen and Robert went every Wednesday and Sunday. The poetic lyrics and swelling melodies of southern gospel music filled Robert's soul. He loved the sound, the feel, and the emotional effect it had on an audience. Harold Lewis, the choir director, instantly recognized Robert's talent. Maureen was so proud that Mr. Lewis had taken an interest in her son. Robert became the youngest member of the choir. She could see her son's eyes light up when Mr. Lewis praised him. Robert had no other positive adult men in his life. She watched as her son leaned on Mr. Lewis for guidance and affirmation. Mr. Lewis groomed Robert for a regional vocal competition. Hours were spent choosing the right song and working on dynamics and presentation. Mr. Lewis insisted on picking up all the expenses for the trip to the talent contest.

Maureen was overwhelmed by his generosity.

"Your son is a one-in-a-million talent. I just want to bless others with his voice," Mr. Lewis explained.

Robert had never been more than five miles away from home in all his twelve years. He was excited to be traveling with Mr. Lewis to the big city of Jackson, Mississippi . . .

Bobby leaned back in the booth and looked out the window. "I don't feel like reading anymore. I don't think we need to go over such ancient history,"

"The lies that were told to you by yourself and others had a significant impact on your choices," Sonny said.

"The lies were told to me by the church!" Bobby blurted out. The page in front of him had an image of Harold Lewis lying in a pool of blood, clutching his neck.

"The church didn't lie to you. Harold Lewis did," Sonny said, softening his voice. "But you lied to yourself when you said that this betrayal didn't matter."

Bobby averted his eyes from the image of the blood-soaked choir director. He cast his gaze out his window. The magnificent view went unnoticed as he recalled that fateful day.

NINETEEN

"THERE WAS no vocal competition in Jackson," Bobby said quietly.

Sonny drove along the high mountain road. Bobby's voice quivered as he reopened the old wounds.

"Mr. Lewis had me practice in the car. We drove for hours singing my song. We laughed and talked. I was so excited. We stopped at an isolated rest stop along the highway. We were going to have a picnic lunch. I noticed there was only one other car at the far end of the large parking area. Mr. Lewis told me we needed to wash our hands before we ate. When we got to the bathroom, Mr. Lewis threw me into a stall and started tearing at my clothes. He had the look of a wild animal on his sweating face. The more I resisted, the angrier he became. I clawed at the breast pocket of his suit jacket. I pulled out a writing pen and stabbed him in the side of the neck. He clutched his throat and slid to the floor. I reached into his jacket and stole his car keys. I ran out of the bathroom screaming. A family that was picnicking on the far side of the park ran toward me. Mr. Lewis staggered out of the bathroom. He collapsed on the sidewalk in front of the shocked family. I started the car and screeched out of the parking lot. A highway patrolman pulled me over two miles down the road."

Bobby stopped reading. Tears were streaming down his face.

"The church didn't attack you at that rest stop. That was the work of Harold Lewis," Sonny said.

"The church hired him. That makes it their fault!" Bobby yelled.

"Look, Bobby, there are a lot of things I don't like about churches, but this isn't one of them. The First Church of the Gospel was just as shocked as you were," Sonny said.

"How do you know?" Bobby asked.

"It's all written in your book," the boy answered.

Bobby blinked away the tears and looked back at the page and continued reading. Harold Lewis was rushed to the hospital. The highway patrolman that stopped Robert pieced together the story from the witnesses. The choir director went on trial. Robert testified. Harold Lewis was convicted and sent to prison. Robert felt a mixture of guilt and relief. He wondered if it was his fault. He felt sorry for his old friend, while hating the very thought of him.

"One day Harold Lewis will have to read his own book. He will have to answer for that day," Sonny said solemnly.

Shivers rushed up Bobby's spine.

"Will there be justice?" Bobby asked.

"There is always justice here," Sonny said.

Bobby put down his book and slid out of the booth. He moved across to the leather couch. He opened the guitar case. Running his fingers over the instrument brought back many memories. He began to strum. The pages of the tour book continued turning whether he was reading or simply talking.

Robert refused to go back to church after the trial. He isolated himself in his room. His studies suffered as he struggled to erase the horror of the assault. Maureen was now alone to bear her son's sorrow. Carl Langston had left in the aftermath of the trial. He blamed Maureen for dragging Robert to church.

Maureen had bought a red and black guitar at the church's

annual garage sale. She thought it might cheer up her grieving son. As soon as Robert saw the shiny instrument he gleamed. It was the first smile Maureen had seen on his face in months. He instinctively started strumming and picking the strings. He listened to the radio and copied what he heard. Within months, he could play every song he heard. Robert would sit on the front porch as the train passed and play to the rhythm of the steel wheels. At night he could hear the sounds of rhythm-and-blues music drifting across the tracks from the woods. He yearned to find out where that music was coming from.

The guitar gave him a way to escape. He poured his heart and soul into learning to play. Maureen would bribe him into doing his homework by promising him time to practice.

By the age of sixteen Robert had grown tall and handsome. The girls noticed his black hair and sparkling blue eyes. Terrified of rejection, Robert did not pursue their advances. He thought if he could get an opportunity to sing to them that he would be accepted.

Robert had long since ventured across the tracks in pursuit of the music in the woods. At the end of a narrow gravel road, young Robert had come across a roadhouse. He would have assumed it to be an abandoned property if it weren't for the rhythm and blues blaring through its thin walls. He slowly walked past the rusty old cars surrounding the building. Above the front door was a hand-painted sign that read "The Palace." Robert never thought about the fact that he was the only white person in the bar. He was attracted to the music. Late into the night, Robert would play with these fine old musicians. They never asked the age of this young white boy. As soon as they heard him play and sing, they welcomed him into their fold.

The oldest musician was a man by the name of Moses Willis. He took a liking to Robert. He began to mentor this talented young musician. Moses was white-haired and frail. His white beard and tired eyes gave his music credibility. Moses wrote many songs. He shared all his original music with Robert. The young white boy had his first solo performance at the Palace. He was frustrated that he couldn't tell anyone. His mother would forbid him from playing in a drinking establishment. The ignorance of the community would condemn him for playing with what they called "colored" people.

In his senior year there was a talent show at his high school. Robert hoped this would be his moment. He signed up and began telling everyone. Most of his classmates thought he was odd. They shunned the recluse who carried his guitar to school.

When Robert stepped out onto the stage, he grabbed the microphone and said, "Hello! I'm Bobby Lane." He then broke into a rhythm-and-blues song. The auditorium erupted. Girls screamed and rushed to the edge of the stage. He lost the contest but won the hearts of all the young ladies in his high school. All the boys wanted to beat him up. All the schoolgirls wanted his telephone number. Bobby was too embarrassed to tell them that he had no phone at his house.

After graduation, Bobby took a job as night watchman at the Jackson Municipal Auditorium. This job allowed him the time to play his guitar and sing. One weekend he was scheduled to work the Saddle-up Boys concert. The Saddle-up Boys had had a string of country-and-western hits years earlier. They were struggling to stay relevant, as the nation seemed to be longing for something new.

The crowd was filling up the auditorium and the band was in place. The bus was scheduled to arrive by seven. Robert was in charge of bringing the four members of the group to the stage. The clock now read seven twenty. The crowd grew restless, and Robert paced backstage waiting for their bus to arrive.

The phone rang on the wall next to the rear entrance. Robert picked it up. It was that simple call that changed his life forever.

The bus driver had walked to a gas station to make the call. He informed Bobby they'd had a tire blowout and they were going to be at least thirty minutes late. As Bobby hung up the phone, the manager for the Saddle-up Boys was hovering. Bobby looked at this overweight man in his white suit and cowboy hat. Billy Pride had been a circus huckster turned music promoter. His sweaty brow and bulging eyes were in Bobby's face as he turned around.

"Where are they, boy?" Billy Pride huffed.

Bobby explained what had happened. The restless crowd began chanting and stomping their feet.

Billy Pride was beside himself.

Bobby smiled at the nervous promoter and said. "Today is your lucky day!"

"Whatcha talkin' 'bout, son? I have a thousand folks out there that want to see a show!"

"Your boys won't be here for at least half an hour. You need a show right now." Bobby said.

"Tell me something I don't know," said the overweight manager.

Bobby ran to the side of the stage. He took off his coat and tugged up his collar. He leaned down, opened his guitar case, and strapped on his guitar.

Billy Pride waddled over to him. "What do you think you're doing?"

"I'm saving your tail!" Bobby said. He strutted onto the stage and grabbed the microphone. "Hello, I'm Bobby Lane," he crooned.

He started playing an up-tempo version of one of the Saddle-up Boys' hits. The band slowly found the rhythm and the song took shape. The crowd booed and chanted, "Saddle-up Boys!"

Billy Pride was about to pull the plug when something magical happened. Bobby Lane's magnetic presence began to seduce the crowd. He took the familiar songs of the Saddle-up Boys and turned them into his own sound.

The seasoned music promoter had always prided himself on seeing a winner. He had built his career on giving audiences what they wanted. He knew he was watching popular music change before his eyes.

By the time the Saddle-up Boys arrived, Billy Pride had signed Bobby Lane to his first contract.

"That sound is original. We've got to get you some new songs to record," Billy said.

Bobby seized the moment. "I have a bunch of songs I have written."

Billy Pride brought his new boy to Nashville to record. Sunrise Records loved his songs. The fusion of gospel, country, and blues was going to change popular music forever. His first album consisted entirely of songs stolen from Moses Willis.

At the same time the tour book stopped turning pages, Bobby stopped playing the guitar.

"Why did you stop?" the boy asked.

Bobby had no words.

Sonny smiled. "You know, I have studied your career. I was always curious about how you came up with all those songs for that first album."

Bobby turned from the window and noticed the young driver staring through him.

"Why don't you tell me what really happened?" the boy said in a matter-of-fact tone.

Bobby grew restless. "Those songs all came from growing up in Mississippi."

"Those songs made you a multimillionaire within eighteen months. By the time you were twenty-one you owned two houses and fifteen cars," Sonny said.

"Is there something wrong with making money?" Bobby asked.

"It is good when rewards flow to those who deserve them," Sonny said.

"What do you mean by that?" Bobby asked indignantly.

Sonny slowly brought the bus to a stop.

"Why are we stopping?"

Sonny opened the bus door.

"The truth shall set you free," the boy said.

"What? You want me to get off this bus? In the middle of nowhere?"

The young driver looked back. "I want you to answer for all that is in your tour book."

Bobby sat tall and stuck his chin out. "And if I don't?"

The boy's face revealed no emotion. "Confront yourself or get off the bus."

Bobby remembered the last time Sonny stopped the bus. A cold shiver went up his spine. There seemed to be finality to the choice he had been given.

Bobby asked, "You said the truth shall set me free. Are you giving me my freedom by opening the door?"

"The freedom of truth is within your grasp. It is *your* choice."

They sat in silence as Bobby stared at the open door. He looked at the tour book on the table. The page was open to an image of Moses Willis.

Bobby sighed, placed the guitar back in its case, and slid into the booth. "I've never told anyone about Moses Willis."

With that, the bus door closed, and Sonny pulled back on to the road. Bobby began reading his book . . .

Someone knocked on his dressing room door. Bobby Lane was about to make his first appearance on national television. He opened the door. A security guard stood next to his old friend Moses Willis.

TWENTY

"THIS MAN INSISTED ON SEEING YOU," the guard said. "He says it's a family emergency."

"Yes, come in," Bobby said. Moses entered the plush dressing room. Bobby thanked the guard and closed the door. After moments of awkward silence, Bobby took a seat on one of the two couches that faced one another. A coffee table filled with Bobby Lane headshots sat between them.

"Looks like you made it," Moses said, taking a seat opposite Bobby and looking around the dressing room.

Bobby plastered on his artificial smile.

The old man shifted in his seat. Tension hung like a thick fog.

Moses cleared his throat. "The family emergency is real," he said. "My wife's got the cancer. The doctors say she needs treatment. That is going to cost money. I'm here to get twenty-five thousand." Moses sank back in the leather, clearly waiting for a reply.

"I'm sorry to hear about Josie. I didn't know," Bobby said.

"Well, now you do, and you can do something about it," Moses said.

"I don't have access to that kind of money. It's all tied up in stocks and bonds--"

"Well, I think it is time you untie it. This is Josie we're talkin' about," Moses said quietly.

Bobby shot up and paced the room. "Listen, I've got to go on stage in a few minutes. Can't we talk about this after the show?"

"I need an answer now," Moses said.

Bobby avoided eye contact. "How did you get here?"

"All my friends at the Palace got a collection together as soon as we heard you were going to be on television. I traveled for three days on a Greyhound bus. I slept in the bus station. This morning I came over here to the theater. I stood in line for four hours," Moses explained.

"But how did you get backstage?" Bobby asked, secretly wishing Moses would just go away.

"I showed the security guard a picture of us taken at the Palace. Taped to the back was my last seventy dollars. I told him it was a family emergency and here we are," Moses said with a wrinkled smile.

Bobby stopped pacing. He slowly sat on the couch. "Look Moses, I really want to help, but I can't just give you twenty-five grand. My accountant has to review all the outgoing expenditures."

Moses leaned forward in his rumpled suit and rested his elbows on his knees. His eyes narrowed. "Boy, you have made millions on my songs. I could tell the world about your ghost writer."

"I was going to pay you for all the songs once I got established," Bobby said defensively.

"You're going on national television. I think you are established," Moses said, as he looked around the upscale dressing room.

Bobby pulled five crisp one-hundred-dollar bills from his pocket and tossed them on the coffee table. "Just take this for now and I'll get you some more help down the road. It was great seeing you again, Moses, and I'll be praying for Josie." Bobby feigned a grin.

Moses shot to his feet. "I don't want your prayers! I need money!

You owe me, boy!" He kicked the coffee table over. The pictures of Bobby Lane and the hundred-dollar bills scattered across the opulent carpet.

The stage manager opened the door. "Is everything all right, Mr. Lane?" he asked.

Bobby looked up at the pasty man with a clipboard tucked under his arm. "No, everything isn't all right. This man attacked me. Call security and get him out of here!"

The stage manager ran out of the dressing room yelling for security. Within seconds, Moses was hauled out of the dressing room.

"You will pay for this, Robert Langston!" Moses screamed.

The old musician was dragged to the back door and thrown into the alley. In the following months, Moses contacted the press about the authorship of the songs. No one believed him. He wrote letters and made phone calls to the record company. The calls went unanswered.

Josie Willis's slow and painful decline was witnessed by her loving husband and their five children. By the time she died, Bobby Lane had become the single most listened to musical artist the world had ever known. The day Josie was laid to rest, Bobby Lane was being honored at a reception given by his record label. As the Willis family lowered Josie into the ground, Bobby was being given a framed copy of his first gold record.

Bobby stopped reading when he noticed the bus slowing to a stop. He looked out the windshield. Standing in the middle of the road was a young couple. The bus came to a stop, and Sonny opened the doors.

"C'mon," the boy said. "I think you might want to see this."

Relieved by the distraction, Bobby gladly closed his book and followed Sonny off the bus.

"Are we going to pick up some hitchhikers?" Bobby asked.

"No. These people are on this road for a reason. This journey cannot continue until you have talked to these folks."

"Why don't you just drive around them?" Bobby asked.

"Getting around your responsibilities has been a pattern in your life. Maybe you should try something different."

Bobby slowly walked into the middle of the road. Standing in front of him was a young couple. He scanned their faces but didn't recognize them. The man held a guitar in his hand. The young lady held two scrapbooks under her arm.

"Why are you standing in our way?" Bobby asked.

The woman wore a flowing, white wedding dress, her partner a black suit and bow tie.

As Bobby neared, the woman said, "This is how we looked on our wedding day."

She opened one of the scrapbooks. The faded photograph matched the man and woman who stood before him. "I have two scrapbooks," she said. "One is of our life from the day we got some bad news. The other is of your life the day you received the same news."

The groom began playing his guitar. The beautiful bride raised the two scrapbooks over her head and threw them on the ground. An explosion of light rushed out of the books when they smashed against the pavement. Two sets of life-size images sprang up in front of Bobby. On the left, he saw pictures of Josie Willis ravaged with cancer. On the right, he saw pictures of himself receiving the keys to his mansion. Bobby narrowed his eyes at the groom continued playing his guitar. It was young Moses Willis before a hard life had changed him.

The contrasting images were telling the story. As the cancer violated Josie, Bobby Lane's fame and fortune soared. The song Moses was playing was Bobby's first number-one hit record.

"Please stop!" Bobby pleaded.

The music got louder as the images became larger. Bobby turned and ran.

The youthful bus driver followed on Bobby's heels. "Where are you going?"

"I am taking my own path!" Bobby yelled over his shoulder.

Bobby reached the back bumper. He froze in his tracks. Every-thing behind the luxury coach was gone. The road had disappeared into a black void. Sonny was now behind him.

Sonny quietly said, *"Whoever follows me will not walk in dark-ness, but will have the light of life."*

Bobby stood in silence, staring blankly at the black abyss. Reluc-tantly, he turned and walked back toward the road in front of the bus. The images of Josie became more graphic as the disease ravaged her. The strident contrast between her demise and Bobby's career moved him to tears. Bobby began to tremble. Moses continued singing.

"You can't blame me for your cancer!" Bobby shouted.

The images kept coming. "My money wouldn't guarantee your survival!" he yelled at Josie over the loud music.

Sonny sat down on the front bumper of the bus. He raised his young voice over the increasing volume of the music. "When Moses came to you in that dressing room, Josie's cancer was in the beginning stages. An operation at that time would have saved her life," he said.

"How was I supposed to know that?" Bobby asked.

The youngster walked up next to Bobby. The large flashing images were now swirling around them.

Sonny looked up at Bobby. "You were blinded by greed and ambi-tion. There have been many entertainers that have performed songs that they did not write. You didn't have to lie about it. If you would have given Moses credit, you both would have prospered."

The music grew louder as the images enveloped them.

"Moses! Josie! Please, forgive me!" Bobby screamed. He fell to the ground, covering his head. The images instantly disappeared and the scrapbooks returned under Josie's arm. Moses stopped playing the guitar.

The silence was as deafening as the loud music had been.

Bobby Lane lay in a ball in the middle of the road. Josie, Moses, and Sonny knelt beside him. They put their arms around him.

The boy whispered in his ear, *"For everyone who exalts himself will be humbled, and he who humbles himself shall be exalted."*

Josie stroked Bobby's hair and spoke in a soothing tone.

"I pitied you, boy, as you ran from your pain. I was angry at first. I soon realized that you would have to answer to a higher authority. I was sad that you had closed your heart."

Bobby broke down in tears. Moses took Bobby's face in his hands, wiped away his tears, and softly said, "The burden of carrying that lie defined your life. It cost you loving relationships. It drove you to drugs and alcohol. My hate turned to pity as I watched you run farther and farther from yourself."

"Arise and walk," came the command from behind Bobby.

Bobby looked at Josie and Moses. They were looking past him, smiling. Bobby felt warmth on his right shoulder. He slowly looked to his right. White light surrounded a beautiful being. The familiar face of the boy, Sonny, had transformed. Bobby was now looking into the eyes of a grown man. He reached toward the light. Colors he had never imagined surrounded his hand. Bobby sensed he was touching love at its very origin.

A resonate voice said, "I am the Son. The way, the truth, and the life," He said. The ground rumbled beneath them.

Bobby smiled. He muttered under his breath, "Sonny Elway."

The light dimmed. Moses, Josie, and Bobby slowly stood. Bobby looked into the face of the bearded man. He was wearing a royal purple shirt and white linen pants. His sleeves were rolled up, revealing his burgeoning forearms. He wore open-toed leather sandals on his feet. The casual nature of his outfit made him seem approachable. His presence was intoxicating. Bobby wanted desperately to be close to his new best friend.

Moses and Josie Willis said their goodbyes. The happy couple turned and walked arm-in-arm down the road. Bobby noticed the road ahead led downhill into a distant valley, toward a shining city of gold.

TWENTY-ONE

BOBBY TURNED TOWARD THE MAN.

"Why did you come to me as a boy?" Bobby asked.

"I knew you were angry at the concept of God. I thought you might open up to a boy the same age you were the day your childhood was stolen. *Unless you become a little child, you cannot enter the kingdom,*" He said. He stretched his arms, and Bobby rushed to embrace Him.

"I am so sorry," Bobby mumbled into his chest.

"Your journey is complete," He said as He held Bobby close.

He broke from the embrace and grabbed Bobby by the shoulders. He looked him in the eye with a huge grin. "Do you want to ride into town in the bus or would you prefer horseback?"

"Ah ... I guess the bus," Bobby answered.

"Great!" He said excitedly. Bobby smiled as He watched him jog over to the bus.

"C'mon! I've got a party planned for you. You can drive."

Bobby was still trying to wrap his mind around what he had just experienced. He hopped aboard the bus and slid into the driver's seat. The Son took a seat in the booth. He closed the tattered tour book and kissed the cover.

"Floor it!" He said.

Bobby trounced on the pedal. His head was pushed back against the headrest as the bus streaked down the road. The scenery outside the window became a blur. The highway wrapped around the mountain in a sharp right turn. The bus gained tremendous speed as they approached the turn.

"Yahoo!" Bobby yelled.

Laughter came from the booth behind him. The bus crashed through a white wooden railing. They soared out over the valley. Bobby laughed hysterically as he maneuvered the bus like a fighter jet. The luxury coach swooshed over the city at Mach speed. They circled many times before landing outside the eastern gate.

"Wow! That was a blast!" Bobby said.

A bluesy trumpet solo played as the gates were opened wide.

"Pull right into that large courtyard," He told Bobby.

The bus crept through the massive gates.

"Thanks, Peter!" the Son said, as the gatekeeper waved them through. Bobby stopped the bus. A crowd began to form in the courtyard.

Bobby patted the dashboard admiringly. "What do you have under the hood of this thing?"

"It's higher-powered," He answered with a wink.

They both laughed as they exited the tour bus.

When their feet touched the golden cobblestones, the bus vanished. Bobby gasped.

"You won't need that anymore," the Son said.

The crowd was not there to see a superstar. They were there to welcome the newest citizen of heaven. His eternal neighbors received Robert Langston. The crowd parted. Bobby was escorted down the golden streets. The sky was awash in the pinks and oranges of sunset. The warm colors gave a glow to the buildings and streets.

"I haven't seen a sun in the sky. Why does it look like dusk?" Bobby asked, gazing upward.

"Heaven lights up every time someone decides to join the family," He answered.

The overflowing crowd lined both sides of the street. Bobby was in awe of the grandeur and spectacle of the holy city.

They walked past large acreage and watched a home being built. A group of people were happily working together to complete the beautiful structure.

"That will be your mother's home. Maureen will be along shortly."

Bobby smiled as he watched the workers. He thought of his father. "Is my father here?"

"Not yet. Your new spirit will make that moment known to you."

"How will you deal with Harold Lewis when he gets here?" Bobby asked.

"That is between Harold and me. When that moment comes, I would ask that you be there. Moses and Josie helped you; maybe you can help him," He said.

"Yes, of course," Bobby answered solemnly.

As they turned the corner, they saw a large marquee jutting out from an ornate theater. The marquee had the name Moses Willis on it. The theater faced a big city park, overflowing with people. Buildings lined the park on all sides. The streets were filled with tents selling food from all cultures. At the entrance of the theater a large outdoor stage had been constructed.

"It's the Moses Willis music festival," He said. "He has invited us." Music blared from the stage. People were dancing and singing. Moses and his band were on stage. Moses looked over and saw Bobby and the Son. The music stopped. The crowd quieted.

The Son's voice traveled across the massive crowd.

"Please welcome to the stage, Robert Langston!" He said.

The crowd erupted as Bobby bounded up the stairs. He hugged

Moses. Bobby was handed a guitar and the drummer hit the down-beat. The band kicked into a rocking blues song.

Bobby was in his element and was thoroughly enjoying himself. After he had played every song he had ever known, the group created new music. The crowd stayed to cheer them on. As the festival was winding down, Bobby took a final bow. The Son escorted him off the stage.

"That was awesome! Thank you," Bobby said gleefully. He looked at the Son and asked, "Are you going to be able to hang out with me? I don't know anyone here."

The Son laughed. "This is a pretty friendly place."

"What if I want to just sit and talk to you?" Bobby asked.

"I have been working on that very thing," He said.

Instantly, they were standing on a canyon floor. Bobby recognized the meadow and sprawling oak tree.

"I woke up screaming a tune here," Bobby said.

The three-sided canyon still had the waterfalls and jutting rock faces. The fourth side with the sloping hill had changed. It was now terraced. At the far end of the meadow was a massive concert stage. He looked toward the lake on their right. On its shimmering shore stood a large two-story home. Bobby had always wanted a lakeside retreat. This was beyond his wildest dreams.

"The natural slope of the hill will give you great acoustics," the Son said enthusiastically. "This is going to be a fantastic venue. You can create any kind of concert you would like. Remember, you have access to all the great musicians and performers across time. I let them know this was being built. They are looking forward to performing here in the many upcoming seasons."

Bobby froze. The idea of performing with all the musical greats was overwhelming. But he could already feel his creative juices flowing, warming him. The immense possibilities began flooding his brain. He walked across the concert stage. He looked toward the meadow and up the terraced slope. He imagined the coming crowds.

"I give you the desires of your heart," He said, placing his arm around Bobby's' shoulder. "Please send me an invitation when you get this thing up and running. You've got a lot to do. I will leave you to it."

Bobby watched as a spotlight hit the stage. It enveloped the Son in blinding light. When the spotlight extinguished, Bobby stood alone.

A voice echoed through the canyon. "If you ever want to talk, I will meet you under your tree."

Bobby looked across the meadow in front of the stage and smiled. His guitar and tour book lay under the lone oak tree.

TWENTY-TWO

THE EXPLORER

"The Lord Almighty has a day in store for all the proud and lofty, for all that is exalted (and they will be humbled)."
Isaiah 2:12

THE SHIP HAD FIRED its landing thrusters as the landing pod descended to the planet's surface. Captain "Mick" Jansen prepared for landing.

It had been a hundred and fifty years since the first mission to Mars, and, after many other missions, it had taken seventeen years to send a star craft this far into the universe.

Ecstatic, Commander Jansen peered out the small window. His long mission was about to come to an end.

The Mother ship, Liberty One was equipped with a large living quarters and an exercise room. Houston had tried to design a comfortable home for their crew of fifty. After seventeen years in space, all the entertainment modules and expansive digital library had proven monotonous. The Commander was anxious to be free of his confinement. The protocol had been breached when Commander

Jensen told his crew that he was going to be the first to land on this planet. Liberty One had been orbiting for three days looking for the optimal landing place for their many supply pods. Impatient, the Commander scanned an area of the planet he thought met all the parameters. He hopped in an exploration pod anxious to plant a flag on the surface of this new world.

A flashing red light on the panel above his head indicated a problem--he was coming in too fast. The landing gear was not engaging. The exploration pod broke through the atmosphere.

Commander Jansen went through his checklist. The extensive training and countless drills had not prepared him for the reality of this situation. He desperately searched for a place to land. To his left, he saw a large body of water. He veered left.

The scorpion-shaped pod hit the water and began flipping across its surface. The sheer force of the ship's speed turned the craft into an exploding fireball. Fifty years of planning and seventeen years in flight had brought Liberty One this far. The planet with three moons buried its first visitor in a deep and watery grave.

When Commander Jansen opened his eyes, he was clinging to a piece of driftwood washed ashore. Waves splashed against the rocks in front of him.

Jansen sat up and leaned against the drenched log. Flocks of seagulls circled above him. The lonely explorer ran his fingers through the white sand. Staggering to his feet, he noticed his flight jumpsuit had not been ripped. He patted his limbs, checking for damage. There was no sign of injury.

The Commander immediately began dictating data to the communication device implanted in his neck when he became a star pilot. Instinctively, he tapped the side of his neck and began making his report to Liberty One. After a few sentences he stopped. He again felt his neck. The implanted device was gone.

"Perhaps the pod washed ashore," he mumbled. Jansen scanned his surroundings and saw no sign of wreckage. *Or maybe the inhabitants of this planet have already taken my ship to study our technology.*

He looked up the sheer rocky wall. A red, striped lighthouse stood atop the cliff. Behind the lighthouse was a white home built in the Cape Cod style of early 20th-century Earth. He was confused; questions raced through his mind as the seagulls and ocean waves continued their duet.

The Commander climbed up the wet mountainside toward the lighthouse, surprised he could so easily scale the rocky wall. He reached the top with ease and stood on thick green grass. The tall striped lighthouse and white house stood watch over the incoming waves. Jansen looked out over the shimmering ocean. The fresh sea air filled his lungs. A feeling of freedom swept over him. His seventeen-year confinement was in stark contrast to these wide-open spaces.

He walked cautiously toward the lighthouse. As he approached the wooden door, his training kicked in. He reached for his eliminator that had always been a part of his uniform. Apparently, the indigenous people must have confiscated his weapon. He waited for the door to slide open. Nothing happened. He looked at the knob and remembered learning about a locking mechanism that would open a door by simply turning the knob. He placed his hand on the doorknob and turned it to the right. The door creaked as it swung open.

He stood in a small office. A large wooden desk was pushed up against the wall. On the desk were charts and nautical maps. A tattered leather-bound book entitled "Commander's Log" sat on a wooden shelf. Two chairs sat facing one another. A single pane window above the desk looked out over the massive ocean. The curious Commander began climbing the wooden stairs that cut through the ceiling on the right side of the room.

The stairs ascended into smaller and smaller right angles. At the top of the stairs was a small space. The railed area was nearly filled by a large light facing the ocean. Four metal pillars held up the roof above their heads.

A white-haired man in a navy blue coat and a ship captain's hat had his back to the commander. Binoculars hung around his neck. He turned around.

"I have been waiting for you," he said in what seemed like an ancient old voice. "When you were still a long way off, I saw you."

Baffled, Jansen made his way around the large metal beacon.

The craggy-faced man stared at him and said, "Now that you have come to the end of your small journey, is it everything you expected it to be?"

The star pilot bristled. "Did you say 'small journey'? I've traveled billions of miles. I spent seventeen years to arrive here."

The old man chuckled and shook his head. "Actually, you have spent your entire life to get to this place."

"I am the first explorer to travel this far into space." Jansen said indignantly.

"Most Commanders acknowledge that without their crew they could not accomplish their mission."

"Of course I meant we."

The old man stroked his beard. "Let me explain to you how far your seventeen-year journey has taken you."

Commander Jansen folded his arms with disdain. "Okay, why don't you tell me?"

The old captain pointed over the rail. The constant rush of waves crashed against the shore.

"Your journey into the far reaches of the galaxy was equal to moving a grain of sand one inch at the bottom of this vast ocean."

"I'm not going to listen to a man whose idea of technology is Morse code!" Jansen sneered.

"Morse code is simple. I think you'll find the most important things usually are," the old sailor said.

"Who are you?" asked Jansen.

"You may call me Captain."

Jansen puffed out his chest. "Well, Captain, on behalf of the planet Earth and the National Aeronautical Space Agency, I want to extend my greetings. I come in peace."

The old Captain didn't seem impressed.

"You come in peace? It looked to me like you came in pieces. Your ship splintered and tumbled into a million fiery fragments."

Jansen instinctively felt the need to defend himself, but he couldn't remember anything about his landing. He only recalled veering left to attempt landing on a large body of water. He remembered approaching the water . . . and then everything went black.

"I woke up clinging to a piece of driftwood," he mumbled. "Wait." He glared at the Captain. "What have you done with my pod?"

"It is in pieces on the bottom of a lake," the Captain said.

"Did you say a *lake*? But I washed ashore on an ocean,"

"That lake is on a planet that is part of another dimension," the Captain explained.

Jansen tried to comprehend the old man's words. "What do you mean by 'another dimension'? Do you mean I traveled through a wormhole or portal?"

"Yes. A portal is a good way to put it," the Captain said.

"What about my ship?" Jansen asked.

"The Liberty one is fine. Your crew is fulfilling the mission without you. On the other hand that little dingy you rode in on has been destroyed."

Stunned, Jansen's mouth went bone dry. It seared his soul that the mission went on without him .He longed to be the first one to plant the flag on the new planet.

Welcome home Mick," the old man said.

The star craft commander stiffened and stepped back against the opposite wall. The giant lighthouse beacon stood between them. "How . . . how do you know my name?"

"Every ship's captain has a log," the Captain said.

Jansen felt his neck. "Why is my communication implant gone?" His eyes widened. "You've removed it and downloaded all my information!"

The Captain smiled. His weatherworn face accentuated his

white beard. He adjusted his cap. "Well ... something like that. I have taken all your vital information and transferred it into a book."

Jansen laughed. "Did you say a book? That makes sense. You wouldn't have the technology to download it!"

The old man gestured toward the stairs. "If I may?"

Jansen stepped aside, and the Captain made his way around the light and down the steep stairs. Jansen rolled his eyes and followed the old man.

They reached the tiny office at the bottom of the stairs. Jansen watched the Captain pick a tattered book off the shelf. The Captain grabbed a chair and walked through the open doorway. Jansen picked up the other chair and followed him. They sat their chairs against the lighthouse wall facing the picturesque home with the white picket fence and rose-covered arbor.

The Captain handed the book to Jansen. "With all your technology, you haven't forgotten how to read, have you?"

"Books have been obsolete for at least a century, Jansen said. "We had an extensive library aboard my ship. All the information is given to us digitally."

"Sometimes it is better to just sit with a good book. The turning of the pages and the smell of the paper are some of life's simple pleasures," the captain said.

Jansen took the book. He looked at it as if it were an ancient relic, because in his world, it was. He had never actually held a book in his hands. He opened the leather cover. The title page read 'Columbus Michael Jansen'. Jansen frowned and looked up at the old man.

"This is your book," the Captain explained.

Jansen looked down at the pages in front of him and started reading.

Columbus Michael Jansen was born on Moon Base Five. Michael and Teresa Jansen, history professors, were given permission to have one son. They were asked to go to the moon base to be a part of the educational department. The limited space aboard the moon base prohibited overpopulation. The couple raised their son with the stories of ancient explorers. The Jansen's loved the sea. They recited portions of 20,000 *Leagues under the Sea* or *Moby Dick* to Columbus every night. Once every two years, the Jansen's received a family vacation to Earth. They would take their son to the seashore. Overdevelopment had destroyed most of the coastlines. National sanctuaries still existed that allowed visitors.

Young Columbus was brought up with historical stories of the famous explorers of the sea. He became intrigued with what the ancient explorers had done. His parents wanted him to pursue a career in oceanic biology.

"You can explore the wonders of the earth's oceans," they told him.

On Moon Base Five, he spent hours identifying the stars and constellations. On the window sill of his bedroom sat a model of the Mayflower. Through its sails he could see billions of stars. Mick Jansen wanted to explore all of them.

TWENTY-THREE

JANSEN LOOKED up from the book. "What kind of technology would allow you to extract such intricate details of my life?"

"When you are ready to receive that knowledge, it will be given to you," the Captain said.

"Listen, Captain! I'm not sure why you spent so much time logging my life. All I want to know is how I can get back to my crew. By now they have set up a temporary landing station. I want to report my findings to Houston and the world," he said.

The Captain leaned his chair back against the lighthouse and pointed toward the book. "Your journey is spelled out in detail in the Commander's Log."

Jansen sighed. "Don't you have anything better to do on this planet than to scan my life and log it into this book?"

The old sea Captain with the weathered, wrinkled face smiled. "I can't think of anything better to do at this moment."

"Are you the only one here? Are you the last remnant of some ancient civilization?"

The Captain gazed at Jansen with wise eyes.

"I am the last and the first; the beginning and the end," he said.

The Captain clearly sensed Jansen's unrest.

"All your life you have sought out new knowledge. You are an explorer. All the answers you seek have been written in your log. Read the pages and explore."

Jansen's mind raced with questions. "Can you tell me about the portal I passed through? You said I crashed in a lake and ended up in an ocean. How is that possible?"

The Captain reached over and passed his hand over the book. The book opened to its final page. Jansen stared down in awe. He wondered why the book obeyed unspoken demands. An image appeared.

"That's the flight recorder from the exploration pod." Jansen said.

The Captain touched the image.

Jansen saw himself going through his safety checklist in preparation for landing. He watched as the pod broke through the atmosphere and then how it veered left toward a large lake. He sat, stunned, watching the pinnacle of earth's scientific achievement hit the water and disintegrate into a fireball. At the bottom of the page he read about the longitude and latitude of where he'd hit the planet, followed by a series of mathematical equations and symbols.

"I have underestimated your technology," Jansen said.

"It is not a matter of technology. What you just saw was the exact account of your transition from the life you had to the life you can have," the Captain said.

"What do you mean by *transition*?" Jansen asked.

"The vessel you had is destroyed," the old man said.

"I know I crashed. You don't have to keep reminding me!"

"I am not talking about the crash. I am referring to your earthly vessel," the Captain explained. "Your body burned when your vehicle exploded on that lake. What you are experiencing now is more real than anything you have ever known."

Commander Jansen had cheated death many times. The memory of his ditching the ship began to surface. His landing gear was stuck.

He had to make a water landing. He remembered the fear of imminent death flashing before him as he first hit the water.

This was difficult to read. He swallowed hard. He began to make calculations. He knew his velocity rating as he roared over the water. There was no mathematical explanation for his survival. He looked at the equations at the bottom of the page.

"What are these?" he asked.

"Those equations represent the exact place in your existence stream when your biological makeup was transitioned into a spiritual entity," the Captain said.

Jansen sat still and quiet for a long while. Finally, he lifted his gaze to the old Captain. "The moment of my death," he whispered.

"It is the moment of your life," the Captain stated.

Jansen sat back against the lighthouse. He looked over the cliff at the large piece of driftwood that lay on the beach below. Jansen tossed the book on the ground. He jumped from his chair. "No!" he screamed.

The seagulls joined his cry as his voice echoed across the water. He ran to the edge of the cliff.

"Why now?" he called. "I've just achieved mankind's' greatest exploratory goal!"

The Captain watched as Jansen paced back and forth on the grassy plateau, the star craft commander desperately trying to make sense of his demise.

Jansen had always relied on science. Numbers never lied to him. He ran the calculations over and over in his head, all while the seasoned skipper listened to him mumble to himself.

After Jansen had exhausted every possible scenario, he fell to the ground. The numbers did not lie. He knew he couldn't have survived the crash.

He ran his fingers through his hair, trying to discern his present surroundings. He slowly rose and stumbled back to the lighthouse. He slumped in his chair beside the old man.

"So, is this where old ship captains go when they die? Looking at you, I would guess your ship probably went down about the time of the Titanic," Jansen said.

The old man chuckled and Jansen joined in. The Captain leaned forward and picked up the book. He tossed it in Jansen's lap. The book flipped open. Jansen was asked to continue reading.

Mick Jansen had enjoyed his youth on Moon Base Five. The log described his adventures in detail. The moon buggy races and exploring the lunar caves with his friends were all a part of his adventures. The family vacations to Earth had always been enjoyable. These getaways always involved the ocean. Young Columbus would stand on the deck of a ship with his father, and they would feel the cool mist of salt water on their faces.

"Columbus," his father would say. "The seas have still not given up all their mysteries. I would love for you to explore their depths."

Columbus insisted his journey would be to the heavens, and he wanted to go farther into space than anyone had ever done. He applied to the Star Academy. He wanted to be the best star pilot the academy had ever seen. Pride drove his ambition. He dreamed his name would be synonymous with his namesake, Christopher Columbus.

Jansen looked up from his book.

"These reasons for my wanting to explore don't seem exactly accurate. I wanted to do this for all mankind. My journey into the universe has brought knowledge and understanding never before comprehended. My weekly transmissions back to earth were watched by millions of people."

The captain looked at Jansen with skepticism. He shook his head. "It wasn't YOUR exploration. Thousands of engineers and scientists spent fifty years developing the technology to allow you to do what you did. You were not after knowledge. You were after fame," he said.

The Captain pointed to the book. Jansen took an exasperated breath and returned to the pages of his life.

Going from Moon Base Five to the Star Academy on Earth was a dream come true. It is there that his reckless behavior began to surface. The cadets were training under water to simulate weightlessness. Cadet Jansen knew the quicker the other cadets washed out of the program, the sooner he could become a star pilot. Growing up on Moon Base Five, Mick had become used to gravity deprivation. The cadets were all tied together as they dived into the ocean. Jansen insisted on diving deep. His dive pulled the other cadets down with him. The instructors were yelling at the group to surface. Jansen kept dropping. Four men washed out that day. One cadet nearly drowned. Jansen denied any wrongdoing. The academy was astonished that he could withstand such depths.

"I was just testing my limits," Jansen explained to the Captain.

"No, you were trying to get noticed by the academy. Do you remember Cadet Wilson?" the captain asked.

"There were a lot of cadets who started that year," Jansen said.

The Captain reached over and touched the page. An image of Noel Wilson stared up from the book. Jansen looked away.

"Do you remember him now?" the Captain asked.

Jansen didn't answer. The image on the page changed and became a picture of Noel Wilson sitting on a chair and being fed by a nurse. The lifeless stare on his face was haunting.

"I heard he had some trouble after he left the academy," Jansen mumbled.

The Captain grabbed Jansen's collar. Jansen flinched.

"Noel Wilson had severe brain damage from a lack of oxygen to the brain. When you insisted on diving deep, Jeremy panicked. He hit the panic button and yanked off his mask. Your ego and ambition caused great pain in the lives of those around you."

"I was pushing the limits to make them better cadets," he explained.

"Tell that to Mr. Wilson's wife and three children who had to live without him," the Captain said.

Jansen jumped out of his chair. The book fell to the grass.

"Why is this any of your business? I didn't travel all this way to be judged by you!"

"Actually, that is exactly why you are here," the Captain said.

Jansen stared at the old sea captain. "I want to ask you again. Who are you?"

"I am the best friend you have ever had."

Jansen looked around. "What is this place?"

"It is not a destination. It is only a small part of your journey," the Captain explained.

Jansen paced the green plateau of grass between the lighthouse and the house. "All the scientific knowledge I've acquired has made me a skeptic. My culture strove to extend the lives of its people. We did that because we were convinced there was nothing beyond the human experience," he said.

"What do you think now?" the Captain asked.

"I don't know what to think. It seems ironic that I would land in water. My parents would be very happy," he said.

"Your parents are very happy," the Captain said.

Jansen spun around. "You've seen my parents?"

The Captain nodded.

"They have already passed through and are fulfilling their destiny," he said.

TWENTY-FOUR

JANSEN THOUGHT about his loving parents. "When they died, I really wanted to believe in a place beyond earth. A heaven or afterlife would have comforted me. My scientific skepticism made that impossible," Jansen said.

The Captain smiled and scratched his white beard. "The yearning you felt for something bigger than yourself was given to you at birth. Spirituality is a part of all humans. The choice to embrace or deny it is yours."

Jansen listened carefully as the Captain continued.

"Your scientific training, and the best efforts of all mankind, moved you from earth to a planet just next door. Decades, even centuries, brought your little craft to smash into a lake. Maybe your scientific knowledge isn't everything you thought it was," the Captain said.

"How long ago did you land here?" Jansen asked.

The Captain smiled, then said, "That question presupposes that there is time. Time only exists within the realm of earth. I have always been here. This specific place was created for your arrival.

This is your transition from one realm to another. It is different for everyone."

"So that's why there's a lighthouse and an ocean. These things were always a part of my upbringing," Jansen surmised.

The Captain pointed toward the house.

Jansen took a closer look at the beautifully manicured home. "That house is an exact replica of the summer cottage my parents rented in Maine. I remember it because it was the last summer vacation we spent together. They had saved and saved in order to rent such a house. That was the best summer of my life. It was also the summer I argued with my father about my future. I dismissed the ancient explorers of the oceans. I thought there was a more important frontier in the stars. It seems like my afterlife should have started in the stars," Jansen said.

"Your desire to reach the stars was based on selfish ambition," the wise old sea Captain began to explain. "It never made you happy. The best summer of your life consisted of spending time with your family."

The Captain rose from his chair. He scooped up the Commander's Log and handed it to Jansen. "Follow me," he said.

Jansen followed the old man to the cliffs. They descended the rocky wall. They arrived near the large oak driftwood that had brought him ashore. Jansen watched the old sea Captain reach out and touch the driftwood. Jansen fell backward on the sand as a beautiful wooden sailboat sprang up. His eyes widened as he surveyed the large vessel. He frowned once he saw the name painted on the side. In gold letters it read, "One Liberty."

Jansen pointed to the name. "Shouldn't that be Liberty One?"

The Captain's face softened. "There is only one liberty. It is in seeking the truth."

The Captain climbed aboard and looked over the side at Jansen. "All aboard!" the Captain hollered while preparing the ship for sailing.

Jansen laughed and climbed aboard. The Captain blew into the sails and the boat began moving out into the ocean. Jansen looked back at the tiny lighthouse in the distance. He was surprised how far they had already traveled.

"Where are we going?" Jansen asked.

The Captain looked back over his shoulder. "We are continuing your journey of exploration."

The salt-water mist on his face reminded Jansen of that last summer in Maine. He lamented the arguments he and his father had had. His parents wanted him to seek out new knowledge. The deep waters reminded him of Noel Wilson. The image of the brain-injured cadet haunted him.

"What ever happened to Noel" Jansen asked.

The Captain pointed to his right. Jansen saw the young man dressed in a cadet's uniform walking across the water.

Jansen panicked. "I don't want to see him!"

The waves instantly swelled. The boat rocked and crashed against the walls of water. The sky grew dark as the rain deluged the wooden deck. Jansen lost his footing, hit his head on the side of the boat, and fell overboard. He began to sink. He thrashed and spit as water filled his lungs. His gurgling screams went unanswered. He reached his hand out of the water in one final attempt to survive.

A strong hand gripped his and pulled him to the surface. Jansen coughed and choked in air. As the waves died down, he was standing face to face with Noel Wilson on the surface of the calm sea. Jansen turned away from Cadet Wilson and attempted to run across the surface of the water.

The sea Captain exhaled a mighty wind, which sent Jansen tumbling back to Jeremy's feet. The handsome young cadet crouched down and brought Jansen to his feet on the surface of the water.

Jansen found it hard to look at him but did so anyway.

Noel said, "The Captain asked me to come and talk to you. That gasping, helpless feeling you just experienced was just a small example of how I felt that day. For the next seventy-two years, images of that horror filled my diminished mind. I ate through a straw and watched my family grow up around me. I died alone in a nursing facility covered in bed sores."

Commander Jansen looked at him, expecting to see hatred or rage. The young cadet only offered his love.

Jansen's shoulders slumped. "I'm so sorry for my actions. I wanted to prove I was the best. My drive to be the best ruined your life. Please, please forgive me, Jeremy."

Noel smiled. "It is not my place to forgive you. Only the Captain can forgive you. I was asked to come and tell you the effects of your actions. I have no animosity toward you. I am just sorry you had to live such a selfish existence," he said.

The cadet looked past Jansen and saluted the Captain. The Captain returned the salute. Jansen watched as Noel Wilson turned on his heels and walked across the water toward the shore.

The Captain maneuvered the sailboat toward Jansen.

Jansen sheepishly climbed aboard.

"Well done, Columbus Michael Jansen," the Captain said.

The sails billowed in the wind.

"Please continue reading," said the Captain.

Once they began sailing across the crystal clear waters, Jansen picked up the book.

Young Jansen continued pushing the limits as a young cadet. A fleet of star flyers was doing maneuvers. The mission consisted of locating a hidden satellite beacon on the moon. They were to land on the lunar surface, find the beacon, and be the first to bring it back to earth. A meteor shower had made it unsafe to complete the exercise. The maneuvers were cancelled. Young Jansen ignored the cancellation. He donned his flight suit and climbed aboard one of the star flyers. The rest of the cadets watched the star flyer lift off the tarmac just as the flight tower hit the alarm. The trip to the surface of the moon through a meteor shower would have been a death sentence for anyone else but Cadet Jansen completed the mission in record time.

The Star Academy expelled him. NASA took notice. They began looking at the reckless young cadet. The risk-taking behavior of the diving incident was among many in their files. His skills were unmatched by anyone. His grades were impeccable. The fact that he was not a team player worked into their unique plans. They had a mission. They now hoped they had their future commander.

Houston recruited the expelled star flyer.

Jansen looked up from his book. "I was so proud when NASA wanted to interview me."

The waves gently splashed against the hull of the boat, and they were moving farther and farther out to sea.

The Captain was at the wheel. He looked over his shoulder at Jansen. "They were not your friends. They had a specific reason for picking you."

"Yeah. I was the most qualified!" Jansen boasted.

The Captain shook his head. "No. I am afraid that's not it. They picked you because they knew you were obsessed. NASA knew they couldn't use you in a conventional capacity. You would get people killed. They picked you because you were reckless and expendable," he said.

"No," Jensen countered. "I became the face of NASA. I was their headline for three years building up to the launch of Liberty One. That doesn't sound expendable to me!"

The Captain listened patiently. Finally, he said, "The fact is, they were not sure that mission would succeed."

Jansen sat stunned, listening to the Captain.

"They implemented the Liberty One project knowing they were not ready. Their funding from Congress would be cut if there wasn't a viable project in place. The Star Academy was their chief rival for appropriations. NASA had become a relic of the past. They needed a project. Liberty One was taken off the drawing board and sold to Washington."

Jansen remembered all the mechanisms aboard his ship that were constantly breaking down. The crew were always using their ingenuity to fix their mistakes. In truth, it was surprising that they made it as far as they did. *The faulty landing gear . . .*

The Captain read his thoughts. "The landing gear on some of the pods were hastily assembled so they could get the project completed. You happen to pick a pod that had not been fully checked. It is a real testament to your crew that they were able to establish a base on that planet against all odds.

"You mean I was a publicity stunt?"

"Yes," the Captain said. "You didn't make it easy on the public relations department. They were trying to sell this great American hero to the press, and you kept messing that up."

"What do you mean?" Jansen asked.

"I mean the more publicity you received, the more outlandish you became."

The Captain pointed at the book. Jansen looked at the open page with an image of a NASA press conference. Jansen began to read.

Commander Jansen strutted into the crowded room. The hot lights and cameras were fixed on the arrogant young star pilot. Questions started coming at him the moment he took a seat. But Mick Jansen was a natural. His charming smile and quick wit made him a media darling.

"Commander Jansen, what do you think you will find beyond our solar system?" came a question from the third row.

Jansen puffed out his chest and smiled. "I'll find that the farther we go into the universe, the less we will have a need for a God. This is mankind's chance to prove once and for all that the heavens are filled with intelligent life, not intelligent design."

The low chatter in the room instantly silenced. The press was used to Mick's press conferences being filled with laughter and great sound bites.

Mick stood and grabbed the microphone off the table. "I will prove to the world that we are not alone. There are other civilizations out there. None of them are in need of a creator. We have created what we have." He dropped the microphone and strolled out of the room.

TWENTY-FIVE

JANSEN LOOKED up from the book. The Captain continued to steer the large sailboat.

"I got a little carried away at that press conference," he said.

The Captain kept steering in silence.

"I should have said I wanted to touch the face of God!" Jansen said sarcastically.

The Captain looked over his shoulder and said, "Your beliefs in the accomplishments of man are interesting. I hope you will come to realize your quest for greatness was in vain."

"Nonsense!" Jansen said. "I have accomplished what NASA didn't even think I could do. Now I am adapting to this new realm. I have done all this without the help of any God!"

The Captain smiled and adjusted his blue cap.

Jansen began to think about being expendable to NASA. He thought about all his friends in the academy. Upon further reflection, he began to realize that the more driven he had become, the fewer friends he had. The cadets relied on one another. No one truly trusted Mick Jansen. He was a loose cannon.

"I just wanted to be the best I could be," Jansen explained.

"Being first to do something doesn't make you the best," the Captain said. "Without friends and family, you do not have much."

"My family always believed in me," Jansen argued.

The Captain slowed the boat. He turned and sat next to Jansen.

"They believed in you, but you didn't believe in them," the Captain said, as the pages rustled forward.

Jansen looked down at an image of his parents . . . The ambitious NASA recruit was training for a preliminary flight to Mars. News came that his parents had died in a boating accident while on vacation off the coast of Maine.

The tragic news came at a time when NASA had given Mick many high-profile responsibilities. They had promised him great things if he would comply with their training regime. NASA had promoted him to the world as the man that would bring them to the stars. On the day of his parents' funerals, Mick was lifting off for Mars. He had convinced himself that exploration was what they would have wanted him to do.

"My parents would have wanted me to explore. That is what they instilled in me as a child," Jansen said.

The Captain nodded. "They wanted you to explore, but they did not want your disrespect."

"I just didn't believe in the God they kept talking about. They taught me to explore. The more I explored, the more I believed in science. The more my parents explored, the more they believed in a creative God. Coming back to earth for some ritualistic ceremony wouldn't have honored them. Funerals are for the living, not the dead," Jansen said.

"I am not talking about the funeral ceremony," the Captain said. "I'm talking about the last eight years of their lives. They tried to contact you. They asked you to come home for a visit. You rarely returned their calls. You thought your legacy was more important than your family."

Jansen noticed the boat had stopped. Three dolphins were dancing on top of the water.

The Captain laughed and said in a cooing voice, "Yes, I see you. We will be right there."

"Why have we stopped? Jansen asked.

The Captain stood. "Just follow the dolphins."

The old man dove into the water. Jansen laughed when the dolphins began squeaking. Jansen dove in after the Captain. They followed the dolphins down into the ocean. Jansen was shocked that he could breathe under water. The panic of drowning was gone. The glistening coral welcomed them as they swam over it. Colorful schools of fish encircled them, urging them deeper into the shimmering depths. A massive whale escorted their descent to the ocean floor. As they swam over a giant cliff, an immense glass house lit up the ocean floor.

The Captain and Jansen set foot in the plush white sand. Jansen looked at the house of glass that stood in front of him.

"Knock on the door," the Captain said.

Jansen floated toward the door. He was about to knock when he saw his parents rushing forward. Michael and Teresa flung open the door.

"Welcome, Columbus!" they said, pulling him into their embrace. "Thank you for bringing us our boy, the most famous explorer that ever lived!" Teresa said to the Captain.

The Captain tipped his hat. "It is my pleasure, kind lady."

"This house was a gift from the Captain," Michael said.

"The Captain gave you this house? How was he able to give you such a magnificent gift?" Jansen asked.

The parents smiled at one another.

"The Captain is able and willing to give you the desires of your heart. You just have to seek the truth," Teresa explained.

They were standing on an upper deck overlooking the sparkling coral on the ocean floor. Jansen looked up. As far as he could see, he saw species of fish swirling playfully in the water.

"Every day is a new adventure," Michael said. "We go out every day and always find new and fascinating discoveries."

Jansen glanced at this father. Wonderment swept across his father's smiling face.

"Where did all this come from?" Jansen asked.

Michael placed his hand on his son's shoulder. "The more we discovered in the earth's oceans, the more we believed in the existence of a creator. After we got caught in that storm in Maine, we arrived here. If we had any doubts, they were quickly abandoned."

"That would explain all the strange things that have been happening," Jansen said.

His parents both laughed.

"Although the journey is different for everyone, I am sure you have experienced some pretty bizarre things!" his mother said with a giggle.

"Oh? You mean like talking to my deceased parents on the deck of their glass house at the bottom of the ocean?" Jansen asked with a big grin. The three laughed and hugged one another.

Michael looked his son in the eye. "The evidence is overwhelming. The fact is, the evidence has always been overwhelming. Exploration of the oceans or the stars results in the same conclusion."

Jansen's scientific logic was still trying to explain his surroundings.

"Stop thinking with your mind; try thinking with your heart," Teresa said softly.

"I will try, Mom," Jansen said.

They rejoined the Captain in the front lobby. The Captain embraced them as they said their goodbyes. Jansen waved down to his parents as they swam toward the surface.

The Captain climbed aboard the One Liberty. He helped Jansen up the side.

"Wow! That was amazing!" Jansen said, taking a seat next to the Captain. "My parents said you gave them that incredible gift. Is that true?"

The Captain nodded affirmatively.

"I don't know why or how you did that, but I thank you. You have given them their dream," Jansen said with tears in his eyes.

The Captain smiled and patted Jansen on the shoulder. Jansen looked across the ocean and then back at the Captain. "My parents were talking and ..."

"Yes? What is it, son?" the Captain asked.

Jansen said, "You have been in this realm for quite a while. What do you think about the idea of a god?"

The Captain stroked his white beard pensively. "I don't think anything of the idea of a god."

"So, you are like me. You need proof!" Jansen blurted.

The Captain smiled. His wind-burned skin seemed to crack. "The idea of a god isn't something I think about. Knowing that God exists is quite a different matter."

"Are you serious? You sound like my parents. You seem very bright and talented. You have acquired the ability to create a glass house or make a boat out of an old tree," Jansen said.

The Captain's eyebrows rose high.

"My point is, you honed and perfected those skills in this new realm," Jansen said. "You have adapted to your environment. All those skills came from you. They didn't stem from some God."

The Captain sat quietly as Jansen explained himself.

"My talents and abilities have always brought me my success. The more knowledge I received, the more I was convinced that I was put on earth to bring the light of knowledge to the world. I always wanted more knowledge, which led to more respect; I set out to prove that it was I, not God, who would explain the existence of the stars. I set out to conquer the heavens!" Jansen boasted.

The Captain shook his head and stood. He walked slowly to the front of the boat. He unfurled another sail and watched as it billowed in the wind. He began to steer the sailboat to the starboard side.

"You remind me of another. Let me show you what that kind of thinking can do for you," the Captain said.

The wind picked up and they whisked across the open sea.

Jansen sat watching the old sea Captain conquering the crashing waves. The book flipped open in Jansen's lap.

"We have got a ways to go. Why don't you continue reading?" the Captain suggested.

Jansen continued to read about his life.

He broke Samantha Collins's heart. They had met in school. Mick and Samantha were the talk of Neil Armstrong High School on Moon Base Five. They continued their relationship when he entered the Star Academy. Samantha followed him to Earth to support his dream of becoming a star pilot. He had promised to marry her. As his reckless behavior escalated, so did his inability to commit to a loving relationship. Mick Jansen loved the idea of having Samantha as his girlfriend. He loved how they looked together. But the young cadet was terrified to settle down. Samantha put up with his infidelity. She hoped he would eventually grow up. She finally wore him down. He bought a ring and they set a date. The wedding that was planned was going to be an event. Samantha had invited everyone from Moon Base Five. Michael and Teresa were so proud of their son. The Jansen's loved Samantha. They would gladly have welcomed her into the family.

The morning of the wedding Mick had a cadet exercise. It was to simulate gravity deprivation in water. He promised his fiancée he would be done by noon. When they pulled Cadet Wilson out of the water, Mick knew there was going to be trouble. He ran away from the scene when the paramedics arrived. By six o'clock that evening, Jansen was suspended pending an investigation. He went into hiding for five days. He couldn't face Samantha or the families. He never talked to Samantha again.

He looked up from the book. The waves had died down.

"Samantha Collins didn't deserve that humiliation and betrayal. I'm truly sorry for what I put her through that day," Jansen said.

The Captain looked over his shoulder as he steered the sailboat. "That's the second time I have heard you admit you were wrong about something. I think we might be making some progress."

TWENTY-SIX

JANSEN THOUGHT AGAIN of Cadet Wilson. He stood up and walked up next to the Captain.

Jansen cleared his throat nervously. "Cadet Wilson said something strange to me back there."

"What did he say?" the Captain asked, as he kept his eyes fixed on the horizon.

"I asked for Wilson's forgiveness. He said forgiveness could only come from you," Jansen said.

The Captain smiled. "Go look in your book. You will find no mention of Cadet Wilson or your wedding day debacle," he said.

Jansen frowned. "I just read about all of that."

"Go look in your book," the Captain repeated.

Jansen turned and walked to the back of the boat.

He picked up the book and began flipping through the pages. He found no references to his wedding day or Cadet Wilson. He looked up. "Did you delete those files?"

"Let's just forget about it. You realized your mistakes. That's good enough for me."

The One Liberty began to slow. Jansen looked toward the shore. "Where are we?"

The Captain looked at him and said, "Do you remember your whole speech about conquering the heavens?"

Jansen nodded.

"That complete arrogance and selfish drive reminded me of someone else. I thought I should show you something," the Captain explained.

The sailboat sailed close to shore. The Captain stepped out of the boat onto the water.

"Aren't you going to anchor the boat?" Jansen asked.

The Captain smiled. "I am the anchor. Let's go," he said.

Jansen hopped out and followed the Captain across the top of the water. Upon reaching the shore, they walked up a rocky ridge. Jansen followed closely behind the Captain. He began to analyze what had been happening to him. His scientific logic was warring with his mother's admonition to think with his heart.

They reached the top of the ridge. Jansen looked out over the destroyed ruins of an ancient city. He followed the Captain through the streets. They walked past toppled pillars. Jansen was awed at the level of destruction.

They made their way under a partly destroyed archway. A mangled iron gate had been tossed to one side on a heap of rubble. He sensed that he shouldn't speak as he followed the Captain through the somber wasteland. They passed a massive gouge in the ground. At the bottom of the hole lay the crumbled remnants of a watchtower.

They approached an enormous hole in the remains of a fortress wall. Jansen followed the Captain as he climbed up the burn-stained breach. When they reached the top, they stood on a mile-wide stone wall. They continued in silence across the wide expanse toward the wall's opposite edge. The Captain suddenly stopped.

Jansen's eyes grew wide and his mouth fell open. In front of him was what could only be described as a tear in the cosmos. The immense wound in the sky revealed no stars or planets. All he could see was a black abyss. He looked at the Captain as the wall began to tremble.

"May your eyes be opened," the Captain said.

A pinpoint of white light began growing out of the old man's chest. Jansen squinted as the warmth hit his face. The cap and white beard melted away. Jansen's knees began to shake as he watched the sea Captain transform into a being of white light. As the light subsided, a muscular man dressed in armor appeared. A shiny breastplate of gold covered his chest and torso. A sword hung low on his side. His knee-high boots were covered in gold and silver armor. A royal robe of purple hung loosely from his broad shoulders. His handsome face was covered with a closely cropped beard. He exuded the majesty of a king.

Jansen fell to his knees. "What kind of alien creature are you?" he cried.

The wall shook as the being answered, "I am the Captain of your salvation. I brought you here to tell you about something that happened before I created mankind. It happened before time itself."

Jansen listened intently.

"I created a beautiful being right here. This was his city. He was the star of the morning. I gave him talent and charisma. I placed him in authority over all the angels. He always wanted more. He wanted to be the greatest in the kingdom. Eventually he wanted to conquer heaven. He wanted to prove that he was the almighty. He drank the blood of pride. His thirst was never quenched."

Jansen sat awestruck watching the warrior gaze out over the rubble. Speaking with the authority of a commanding general, he told of the battle of heaven.

"This is where the final battle for heaven took place. We had him flanked on three sides. His army consisted of one-third of all the angels. We drove his army back to this very spot." He pointed toward the massive hole in the sky. "That is where I crushed his armies and tossed them out of heaven!"

He pulled his sword from its sheath. He raised it over his head and drove it into the top of the wall. Golden white light shot out in all directions. "The fallen angel is not allowed past this sword. He slithers up onto this wall every day. He runs back and forth in front of the sword accusing each of my children by name. He assumes if he keeps telling me their faults, I will eventually concede that their creation was a mistake."

Jansen was reeling. The transformation of the Captain and the explanation of the destruction around him was so much to absorb. "I always thought the story of Lucifer was just mythology," Jansen whispered. He faced the ancient warrior standing on the wall. "I never believed in you, sir. Do I call you God?"

He smiled at Jansen as He lifted him to his feet.

"God is what I am. Just call me Father. I would like that," He said.

Jansen gazed out across the war-torn landscape. "You knew the revolution was about to take place. Why didn't you stop it? Wouldn't that have saved all this destruction?"

The Father gestured over the crumbled city. "This is just a fraction of the destruction. I have restored the rest. To answer your question, I wanted to give them every chance to come back to me. At last I just had to release them," He explained.

"Do you know what started the uprising?" Jansen asked.

The Father nodded. "He was there when we decided to create the human race. I was discussing my plans when he came into our presence. He was incensed. He knew that he was the most beautiful creature I had ever created. I was discussing the creation of a being that was above the angels. I wanted to create a people that were made in my image. That was the beginning of his revolt."

"Why do you keep all this in ruins?" Jansen asked.

"It is an eternal monument to pride. I have left it here for cocky young bucks like you. You told me you wanted to conquer heaven to prove there was no God. You wanted to exalt yourself above any concept of a creator. Take a good look around, Mick. This is the ultimate result of that way of thinking."

Jansen finally understood. "My whole life I pursued one goal. I wanted to be the most famous explorer that the world has ever known. All the tools I had to achieve my success were given to me by you. I twisted my gifts to achieve worldwide fame." He sat down on the edge of the wall and faced the horrific rip in the sky. He then looked at the Father. "I don't want to be cast out of heaven."

The Father sat next to him and put his arm around him. "I will never leave you or forsake you."

They sat in silence as Jansen basked in the total acceptance of his newfound friend.

The Father stood and unhooked the golden breastplate. He leaned it against the sword. "Lucifer cannot pass the breastplate of righteousness," He said with authority.

Jansen slowly walked around the sword and breastplate. He followed the Father off the wall and through the devastation. They walked for many miles. When the wreckage of the mighty war was far behind them, the Father took Jansen on a small tour of heaven.

"This is only a microcosm of what has been created," the Father said. "The good news is I am always creating, so you will always have new places to explore!" The Father smiled.

Jansen was in awe of all that he was experiencing.

With a twinkle in his eyes, the Father said, "You know you can now fly without having a big metal scorpion wrapped around you."

Jansen thought of the fifty years it took to build the Liberty One project. He reflected on the seventeen years in flight. It all seemed so insignificant now.

TWENTY-SEVEN

"LET me give you some heavenly perspective," the Father said to Jansen, pointing toward the valley below.

Jansen saw a black mass floating in a meadow. At the far end of the clearing was a large barn surrounded by a thick forest.

"That barn is my workshop," He explained, as they descended into the valley.

As they got closer, Jansen sensed that the black mass was a living entity. Its rounded shape seemed to sparkle with each ebb and flow. Jansen calculated the black floating energy was approximately one hundred feet in diameter. He stood amidst the wildflowers gazing at the twinkling mass. A beautiful white horse stood in the distance. The majestic animal appeared content to graze on the thick green grass beneath him.

Jansen slowly circled the mass. "What is this beautiful creation?"

The Father reached his hand inside and unfurled his fingers. The mass expanded and they were now enveloped in the sparkling darkness.

The Father pointed at a small spec of light in front of them. "Do you see that star?"

Jansen nodded, unable to speak.

"Look closely at the third little blue light that encircles it."

Jansen found the tiny blue spec of light.

"I found it!" Jansen said enthusiastically.

"That is Earth circling the sun," the Father explained.

Jansen stared at the blue dot peacefully circling the white speck of light.

The Father said, "If you look about three hands to your right, you will see the planet where you crashed your pod."

Jansen was in silent awe. The Father closed his fingers. They were standing outside the mercurial mass.

"That is the entire universe," the Father said.

Jansen walked around it several times. He laughed and couldn't stop. Finally, he caught his breath. "I guess I sort of underestimated your technology.

The Father chuckled. "'Ya think?'"

They both broke out in laughter. The Father pointed toward the large barn. "That is where I created mankind. I still remember the day I created someone called Columbus Michael Jansen."

Jansen smiled. "Well, that was a banner day!"

The Father placed his hand on Jansen's shoulder. "Do you want to fly without a ship?"

Jansen felt exhilaration swell inside him. He had always loved to fly. He nodded.

The Father smiled mischievously. "Hang on."

The two shot up into the sky at the speed of sound. The whooshing sound made the white horse rear up on his hind legs and whinny. They dived into the valleys and over treetops. Jansen was ecstatic. As soon as he thought they couldn't go faster, they would find another level of speed.

They finally arrived at the eastern gate of the city. Peter opened the gate, and Gabriel blew his horn. The Father and Jansen gently landed. They walked under the massive arch.

The Father put his arm around Jansen and announced, "Please

welcome Columbus Michael Jansen, the explorer who finally found what he was searching for."

Billions cheered. Festive music played. The Father escorted him through the golden streets as the crowds welcomed him home.

A private dinner was held in the home of Christopher Columbus. The guest list included all the great explorers across time. Jansen and his parents reveled in the stories of Columbus and Magellan. Lewis and Clark and Neil Armstrong sat with Jansen at his table.

The Father stood to make a toast. "Raise your glasses to a man who found out that wherever you go–there you are!"

Everyone laughed and cheered.

Commander Jansen thanked Christopher Columbus for his hospitality. As they strolled away from the dinner reception, Jansen sensed the Father had another surprise in store for him.

"Where are we going now?" he asked the Father.

"I am sending you home."

Jansen quickly looked around. They were standing in the lighthouse, overlooking the glistening sea. "What are we doing back here?"

The Father looked down at the crashing waves. "I want to assign some duties to you."

"Reporting for duty, sir," Jansen said, saluting.

The Father smiled. He looked Jansen squarely in the eye. "Your purpose on earth was to tell the world about me. I gave you the talent, the platform, and all the evidence."

"I'm sorry, sir. I didn't see you," Jansen said.

The Father's eyes brightened. "Your purpose continues. You now have eternity to tell the story. I am going to give you some explorers who are lost. They will be drawn to my light from this lighthouse. They will wash ashore clinging to a tree. Their trees will be planted throughout the kingdom. All their journeys will be different, but they will start from this point. Tell them your story. Show them hospitality in your new home. I will reveal myself to them when it is appropriate."

"Thank you, sir," Jansen said. "I'm honored."

The Father smiled and placed his hands on Jansen's shoulders. "Whenever you need to talk, I will be here."

A salty sea wind hit Jansen's face. He found himself sitting on a large piece of driftwood on the beach where he had first washed ashore. He gazed up the steep cliff to see the lighthouse and Cape Cod home above him. The leather-bound Commander's Log lay open in his lap. An inscription on the first page brought a smile to his face. It read: "Mission Accomplished, Commander Jansen. One small step for God, one giant step for Mick!"

Jansen closed the book and slid down onto the sand. He leaned against the driftwood and ran his hand over the letters "One Liberty" carved in the wood. The seagulls and crashing waves welcomed him home. A sense of adventure surged through him, as he realized his journey had truly just begun.

TWENTY-EIGHT

THE THIEF

"He who loves silver will not be satisfied with silver; Nor he who loves abundance, with increase. This also is vanity."
Ecclesiastes 5:10

THE AFTERNOON SUN BEAT DOWN. He desperately needed water. Pain and thirst were fighting for control of his mind. He didn't want a sponge filled with vinegar. That's what the Roman soldiers had given the man hanging next to him.

The thief's hands were nailed above his head on a crossbeam. His feet were nailed to a stake. He realized the only way to breathe was to push downward on his feet. This painful act gave him enough leverage to gasp for one more breath. With every push, more flesh was torn from his feet.

There were three being crucified that day. Two were criminals. The third man was charged with being a threat to Rome.

The convict on the far side was yelling and swearing at the soldiers. The bloodied man in the middle was strangely quiet. The thief remembered seeing the quiet man preaching in Jerusalem. So what could he have done to deserve this?

The criminal on the far right began to taunt the man in the middle. The man did not respond.

Compelled to defend him, the thief shouted, "We are sinners! We deserve this punishment. This man has done nothing wrong!"

The man in the middle struggled to breathe. The thief looked at him and pleaded, "Remember me when you come into your kingdom."

The battered man cast his gaze toward him. He looked the thief in the eye. "*Surely I say to you, today you will see me in paradise.*" He gasped.

A steady calm came over the thief as he choked out his last breath.

When he opened his eyes, he was leaning against the trunk of a gnarled oak tree. The tree sat atop a large grassy hill. Two men were walking up the hill, heading straight for him. He was struck by how much they looked alike. The only thing that separated them was their clothing. The man on the left wore a multicolored robe that seemed to change colors with each step. The one on the right wore a luminescent white robe.

The man in white said, "My son told me you were coming. Welcome to paradise, Andrew."

Startled the man knew his name, he found it hard to look the man in the face. But something in his wise-looking eyes seemed to touch Andrew's soul.

The man in the ever-changing colorful robes approached him. He placed his hand on Andrew's shoulder, instantly comforting him. He felt an immediate kinship to the twins because he, too, had grown up with a twin brother.

The man in white exuded a fatherly strength, while the man in colorful robes had a comforting spirit. The twins seemed inextricably linked.

"Where am I?" Andrew asked.

"My son promised you paradise," the man in white said.

Andrew remembered the hot sun, the torturous pain, and the unbearable thirst. He recalled the gentle, bloodied man who had promised to see him again.

Andrew looked down. He was wearing different clothes. He now wore a brown-and-burnt-orange-colored robe. His leather sandals were comfortable and new.

The holes in Andrew's hands and feet were gone. The broken rib given to him by the Roman soldier, healed. He fell back against the tree. "What has happened?" he asked.

"You have been given what he promised," said the fatherly twin. Andrew looked around at his surroundings. He could see a beautiful city down in the valley below. A large male lion was sleeping alongside a delicate lamb on the grassy slope of the hill. His will to survive and compulsion to steal had somehow been lifted, and he no longer felt any inner struggles.

"Do you mean paradise?" Andrew asked.

"Yes," said the comforting one. "You took your last breath. You are no longer a part of that world."

Shocked, Andrew asked, "Who are you men?"

The man in white smiled and answered, "I am the Father and this man is the Comforter."

"Where is the man who promised to meet me in paradise?" Andrew asked.

"If you have seen us, you have seen him," they answered in unison.

"But . . . I can't be dead," Andrew said softly. He slowly sat on the soft green grass under the tree.

"He was visiting Jerusalem saying he was the Son of God. I think that is what got him killed."

A mournful look swept across the Father's face. "Many did not want to receive the gift."

"He seemed like a kind man," Andrew said. "He sure didn't deserve the punishment he received. Did he make it to paradise?"

The Comforter patted Andrew on the arm. "He IS paradise."

The three sat back against the trunk of the old oak.

"He was who He said He was," the Father said proudly.

"Do you mean the Son of God?" Andrew asked.

The Father and the Comforter nodded. "In whom I am well-pleased," they said together.

"If that is true, then where is he?" Andrew asked.

The Comforter explained, "Time and space do not exist here. From the moment you took your last breath, until now, three days and nights have passed on earth. He has not yet ascended to the Father."

The Comforter reached into his colorful robe. When the front of his robe opened, shards of light shot in all directions. He pulled from the light a leather-bound book.

The Father said, "This is your book. We have been writing in it long before you were born."

The Comforter reached into his robe for a second time. Brilliant colors flashed in Andrew's eyes. He brought forth a scroll.

"We have been planning for this moment," the Father said.

Andrew watched as the Spirit unrolled the white scroll.

"These are some of the plans we drew when we decided to create you," he explained.

Andrew looked at the unrolled parchment with highly technical drawings of his face and body. In the margins, intricate details about how he would walk and the timbre of his voice were all neatly inscribed.

"Is all this about me?" Andrew asked.

The Comforter smiled. "You were wonderfully made."

Andrew sat speechless. The hand-drawn plans described him perfectly.

"We drew these plans when Adam still walked the earth," the Father said.

The Comforter rolled up the scroll and tucked it back into his robe.

The Father picked up the book and handed it to Andrew.

"We need to talk to you about the pages of your life."

Andrew was still trying to rationalize what was happening. He rubbed his fingers through his beard and mumbled, "I woke up under this tree and you two greeted me. Then you spoke about plans and books written about me." Andrew pointed at the Spirit and said, "I don't know if you know it, but your robe seems to be on fire. Every time you open it up, I get blinded with light."

The Father and Spirit laughed.

The Father said, "The crucifixion took your life. My Son noticed your willingness to believe in Him. He promised He would see you again."

The Spirit passed his hand over Andrew's book. The book opened to the final page. Andrew looked down and began reading about his final hours on the cross.

The last line in the book read, "Andrew, son of Bartholomew, choked his last breath as the Son promised he would see Him in paradise." Symbols and numbers he did not understand followed.

"I never believed in a paradise. I thought all that Jehovah stuff was just religious fantasy," Andrew said.

"How do you explain what you are experiencing now?" the Father asked.

"I can't explain it. All I know is that I don't feel dead. Look at me. I have new clothes. I have no scars. I am fine and well!" he said.

The Comforter chimed in. "As you drifted between here and there, you had visions. You saw the spikes being pulled out of your hands and feet."

The Father asked, "Do you remember looking down on yourself as you hung in the hot sun?"

Andrew sat in stunned silence. The Comforter smiled and looked deep into Andrew's eyes.

"You fell into my arms. I gently placed you at the foot of the cross. The Roman soldiers didn't see us. They were carrying your physical body away when you awoke under this tree," he said.

Andrew's memories began to stir. He remembered drifting in and out of consciousness. He recalled feeling like he was at an entrance to a door that seemed to open and close, as his life and death fought for existence. He had thought those memories were a result of the pain and exhaustion. Now he wasn't so sure.

"I have lived a deplorable life." He sighed. "How can I be given paradise?"

Father replied, "My Son promised He would see you here. He did not promise you paradise."

"What does that mean?" Andrew asked.

"It means you have to answer for your life. The chance to live here will be determined by you," the Comforter said.

Andrew settled back against the tree. He looked at the book lying in his lap. He breathed in the smell of clover and honeysuckle. It reminded him of a late spring day. Animals of all kinds roamed the hills and valleys. Clusters of people were sharing meals on blankets. He watched as one group laughed at a bear cub that was tumbling down the hill. The city in the distance glistened. Thoroughly distracted, he watched as people entered and left the city on a wide road.

"You will have an opportunity to experience all paradise has to offer, but first . . ." the Father tapped on the book. "We have some business to attend to."

Andrew nodded and began to read.

Andrew, son of Jacob, was born in Nain. His mother, Rebecca, had given Jacob two boys and seven daughters. Timothy and Andrew were twins. Andrew was born second. His father was a tent maker. Jacob began teaching his sons the family business. Andrew's enthusiastic older brother learned the trade. As firstborn, Timothy stood to inherit two-thirds of his father's estate.

"Someday all this will be yours," Jacob would tell his firstborn son. When Andrew and Timothy were alone, Timothy would always taunt the younger twin.

"When father dies, you will get nothing from me! This family will serve me," Timothy would say.

As Andrew grew, he began to resent the elaborate tents being made for the affluent.

"We toil for weeks on these fancy tents, and they pay you with the leftover coins in their pockets," Andrew would say to his father.

"The Lord has provided this family with a skill that sustains us. We are doing quite well. God has blessed us, my son," Jacob would say. Andrew loved his father but thought he was foolish. He watched the family working together, making tent after tent. Andrew wondered why the rest of the family didn't see the futility of their efforts.

Discontentment burned inside him. He knew he could find a better way. He yearned to tell his father the truth about his older brother. But he knew he wouldn't be believed.

TWENTY-NINE

ONE MORNING when Andrew was in his late teens, his father asked him to take a trip to the market in Jerusalem. Twice a year Jacob would go to see the different fabrics and colors being offered. He would meet with existing and potential customers. Andrew resisted the invitation.

"Why don't you take Timothy? He is the one who will be running this business," Andrew said.

Jacob patiently smiled at his son. "I am asking you because I want to teach both my sons the ways of the market. It is something you will need to know."

Timothy had heard his father tell the stories of the market many times. As the family worked together sewing the tents, Jacob would try to instill his experience to his sons.

Andrew and his father loaded up the donkeys and headed toward Jerusalem. Jacob knew a short cut over Mt. Tabor. It would take time off the journey. The seasoned tent maker was anxious to get to market. Along the way, Jacob talked to his son. He told Andrew the dreams he had for him. He spoke proudly of his firstborn. He assured

Andrew that Timothy would make him an integral part of the business.

Andrew rode in silence. The echoes of his older brother's taunts rang in his ears.

The hot sun beat down on them as they approached a steep embankment. The animals were loaded down. The extra weight made them skittish as they began to descend into the ravine. The spring rains had washed away some of the solid ground. Loose gravel and jagged rocks were all that remained. The only other route would take them days out of their way.

"Perhaps we should get off the donkeys and lead them down the hill," Andrew said.

"Son, I have traveled this road twice a year for many years. This ravine is always a little scary after the spring rains. We have to get to the city by tomorrow. I have customers awaiting my arrival," Jacob said.

The stubborn old man began his descent. Andrew was afraid. But his father insisted that dismounting would take too much time.

"Be a man!" Jacob yelled at his son.

Tentatively, Andrew began to follow.

Fear overtook him. Andrew tried to retreat back up the steep gulch. He kicked his donkey in the ribs and pulled the reins to the left. The donkey began to turn and the rocks slipped under them.

The weight of the packs, coupled with the steep incline, proved too much for the animal. Andrew leaped from the donkey as it toppled onto its side. Andrew smashed against a large ledge. He clawed his way up to the safety of the rock shelf. When he looked down, he saw an avalanche of boulders and pack animals cascading down the ravine.

The dust settled at the bottom of the hill. His donkey had survived and was getting on its feet. Andrew saw his father crushed in the midst of the rubble, lodged under his own donkey.

"Father!" he cried out. Andrew jumped off the ledge. He landed on the loose shale and tumbled down the hill. He clawed at the rocks, trying desperately to get to his father. The last rock he pulled away was bathed in blood. His father's skull had been crushed.

Andrew dropped the rock and screamed at the heavens. For hours he sat next to his father, rocking back and forth. Waves of grief and fear hit him over and over again. He knew what awaited him when he returned home.

He rummaged through the leather bags that were strapped to the donkey. There were provisions for the trip and a purse filled with coins.

Andrew buried his father with rocks, then mounted the surviving mule and headed for Jerusalem . . .

"I didn't know what else to do. I felt so trapped," Andrew said, as he looked up from his book. "I stole my father's money to survive. I was just a stupid child."

The Comforter said, "The money belonged to the family. Rebecca and Timothy could have used that money to provide for the rest of your siblings."

Andrew felt guilty that he had not returned the money to his mother. "I was afraid to go home. My brother had promised to enslave us."

"You had no faith in your mother. She is a wise woman. Her strength and understanding of Timothy would have manifested itself," the Father said. He gestured to the book. Andrew continued reading.

The seventeen-year-old Andrew entered Jerusalem as a scared and grieving child. His sheltered life at home was over. He knew he would have to rely on himself to survive. As Andrew walked through the streets of Jerusalem, he felt a mixture of fear and excitement. For the first time in his life he was free to do what he liked. He no longer had to be a tent maker. He wondered what he wanted to become. Andrew dreamed of ways to spend all that money in his father's purse. The things the city had to offer overwhelmed him. His father talked only of the market. Jacob had never told his sons of the other opportunities that await a visitor to the city.

There were places he could go and drink all the wine he wanted. They had women there that would be very affectionate as long as he kept spending money. He noticed that as long as he spent money, he had many friends.

Within six weeks, his riotous living had taken his donkey and all his father's money. Andrew was destitute. He recalled his father speaking of his many loyal customers. One name was always at the top of that list: Benjamin, a very wealthy merchant. Andrew's family had created many tents for him. Andrew knew his father had gained his trust. This gave Andrew an idea.

The market was just as his father had described, a large courtyard filled with tents and tables. The smell of spices and perfumes filled the air. The sound of chattering negotiations and wind chimes surrounded him. Andrew asked many people if they had seen the famously rich merchant named Benjamin. He finally made his way to an elderly woman selling her pottery. The midday sun was beating down. The old woman shaded her eyes as she looked up at Andrew.

"Benjamin just purchased a vase from me. He is in town all week buying things for his new home," she said, squinting at the young inquisitor.

"Thank you so much," Andrew said.

He rushed back into the crowds. His father had described Benjamin's appearance over the years. He was a squatty man who always dressed in bright colors. He wore a lot of gold bracelets and necklaces. Andrew thought he could probably spot him in the crowd. While milling through the last aisle of tents and tables, he saw him.

Benjamin was looking at rugs. His graying hair and beard were neatly combed. He was dressed in a bright red robe with a wide gold belt wrapped around his abundant middle. His smiling face was inviting as he perused the many rugs on display. He had four servants following him. They were carrying baskets filled with his purchases.

Andrew cupped his hands, hoping to be heard over the crowd.

"Benjamin!" he hollered.

The rotund man spun around. His gold bracelets jingled on his wrists.

"Yes? It is I," he said.

Andrew stood up straight and cleared his throat. "I am Timothy, firstborn son of Jacob of Nain. My father wishes to extend his apologies. I know you have been expecting him."

Benjamin tilted his head. He stared at the boy for a long while.

Andrew's knees shook under his robe.

"What has happened to Jacob?" Benjamin asked.

Andrew shifted his feet. He looked Benjamin in the eye and approached him. "My father's business is expanding. He has many new customers. He wanted to be here in person, but since his business is demanding of his time, he couldn't get away. So, he has sent his firstborn son to meet our most valued customer."

With that bit of flattery, Andrew bowed.

Benjamin smiled broadly.

"Jacob has told me of his family, and especially of his firstborn son, Timothy. How do I know you are who you claim to be?"

Andrew swallowed hard. He flashed Benjamin his best smile. "My father told me of your shrewd business sense. Last year we were honored to produce for you the blue-and-white-striped tent with gold fringes. We embroidered your name above the front entrance. It was one of our most beautiful creations."

He hoped his firsthand knowledge of the tent would be enough.

Suddenly Benjamin reared his head back and laughed. "Timothy! Son of Jacob!" proclaimed the rich merchant. He held out his arms.

Andrew followed his lead and ran and hugged Benjamin. "It is truly a great honor to finally meet you," said Andrew.

Benjamin appeared truly happy to meet him.

"Your family has given me great deals on some beautifully crafted tents. The pleasure is mine," he said.

Andrew stepped back to get a good look at Benjamin. His father had always said that in order to gain a person's trust, you must look them in the eye.

"My father has instructed me to find you. Our family would be honored to produce another tent for you. I understand you have just completed your new home. Perhaps you will need a tent for a party," Andrew said, with his most mature sounding voice.

Benjamin stroked his beard while Andrew continued selling his idea.

"It will be made of the finest materials. Quality and perfection will be sewn into every stitch," Andrew bragged.

Benjamin broke out in a belly laugh. "You are your father's boy! Jacob could always sell me on his new ideas."

Andrew's pulse quickened. He asked Benjamin for the standard down payment in order to buy materials. Benjamin gladly handed over the money and described in detail how he envisioned his new tent.

The portly man frowned. "Aren't you going to make any notes?"

Andrew knew he never intended to make the tent, but quickly replied, "My father has taught me well. I will remember," he said.

Andrew promised Benjamin a delivery date. They shook hands, and Andrew disappeared in the crowd.

Over the next few months, Andrew repeated the same ruse many times. In his father's parchments were lists of customers. Andrew made promises to them he never intended to keep. The young boy kept spending the money as fast as it came in. The delivery dates on the tents came and went.

"That is how the stealing began," the Father said.

Andrew looked up from the book. "I was hungry and desperate. I only did that to survive."

The Comforter lifted a brow and patted him on the shoulder. "You were desperate for wine and prostitutes."

Andrew was speechless.

"Keep reading, son," the Father said.

Andrew reluctantly turned back to his book.

THIRTY

ANDREW HAD PAID a week's rent on a large room facing the market square. He had just spent three days throwing a party for anyone who would join him. When the wine and food ran out, the party died. One of the guests at the party worked for Benjamin, the merchant. He informed his boss where Andrew was staying. As the front door was being kicked down, Andrew quickly escaped to the rooftop. The reputation of the firstborn son of Jacob was officially ruined, and there were many angry customers wanting to find him.

Over the next year, Andrew's life continued to unravel. His career went from market square swindler to petty thief. He broke into homes to steal jewelry and food. He learned to spend time around large crowds, stealing from purses and carts. He was constantly vigilant. He lived in the shadows of the city. He learned to survey a crowd from an alley or rooftop. He could usually spot his prey. He would wait until they were distracted, and then he would strike.

One day, as he sat crouched on a rooftop, he gasped at whom he saw in the crowd. Timothy, firstborn of Jacob the tent maker, rode his mule into the market square. Andrew ducked behind the small wall that surrounded the top of the building. His thoughts raced. He wondered if his twin brother was looking for him. Andrew got up the courage to peek over the wall. He looked down on the bustling crowd. His older brother was dismounting the mule. Andrew held his breath as his brother now stood directly beneath him. Timothy was approaching a stout white-haired man with gold jewelry around his neck.

Timothy yelled over the crowd, "Benjamin! I am Timothy, son of Jacob, from the town of Nain. I would love to talk to you about our fine tents!"

Benjamin swirled around.

He pointed at Timothy and screamed, "Seize him!"

Andrew watched as four large servants dropped their baskets and pounced on Timothy. Benjamin slowly walked forward as the servants knocked Timothy to the ground.

Benjamin looked down at the young man lying in the dirt.

"I have searched for you, boy!" he said.

Timothy looked confused. He struggled to get away from the grip of the servants.

"Get him up!" Benjamin yelled.

The servants pulled Timothy to his feet. Benjamin grabbed his hair and pulled his head up.

"Why does Jacob continue to try to steal from me? There are others who have fallen victim to your lies. I curse myself for ever trusting your family."

Timothy gasped. He tried to explain. "That must be my twin brother, Andrew. We thought he had died alongside our father."

Benjamin grabbed Timothy by the collar and spit in his face. "You have lied to me for the last time. Your father owes me money. I will take his firstborn son as my slave until you have worked off your debt. When I am done with you, there are many more who will want restitution."

Timothy's hands and feet were tied. He was tossed into the back of a horse-drawn cart. Benjamin instructed his servants to take him home and chain him in one of his barns. The horses pulled the cart through the crowd. Timothy was pleading and struggling to get free.

Andrew watched in horror as his innocent brother was bound and hauled away by Benjamin's servant . . .

"You could have stepped down from that rooftop and saved your brother," the Father said.

Andrew looked up from the book.

"My brother is an evil man. He wanted to enslave our entire family. He got what he deserved!" Andrew said.

"That is for me to decide, my son," the Father said.

He looked Andrew in the eye and said, "You are the one who stole. You are the one who lied. Your brother's threats were only words. He only told you those things because he knew he wasn't ready to take over the business. He thought you were much smarter than he was. Keeping you scared and resentful was his way of controlling you."

"Timothy thought I was smarter than he was?" Andrew asked.

"Yes. He didn't believe he was worthy of the rights of the first-born," the Father explained. "Your father was very insistent that Timothy take care of the business. He constantly reminded him of his responsibilities to the family. Timothy cried himself to sleep every night. He lashed out at you out of fear, not evil," the Father said.

"Your selfishness and resentment brought you the life you created for yourself," the Comforter said.

Andrew couldn't speak as he realized that his resentment over being the second twin had been a source of bitterness his entire life.

Andrew cleared his throat. "The truth is, I wanted my father to shower me with all that attention. I knew I was only a few minutes younger than Timothy. Those few minutes meant everything."

Andrew returned to his tattered book.

The image on the page was of another crowd in Jerusalem. It had been over a year since his brother had become Benjamin's slave. The other powerful men that Andrew had swindled wanted Benjamin's slave dead. They were angry that Benjamin had found the thief first. They pleaded with him to give them their revenge.

There was a young rabbi in and around Jerusalem that had been gaining a following. Andrew followed him, hoping to steal from his followers. He heard the young man speaking as he slithered through the crowds looking for his next prey. The young teacher's voice mesmerized his listeners. Andrew knew this man was not a charlatan. His words seemed sincere, and his message was simple.

The temple had become another marketplace in Jerusalem. Affluent merchants and landowners would come to buy and sell. The large crowds attracted Andrew. He waited in the shadows at the entrance of the temple. His head covered, he sat near the stone steps. He noticed Benjamin's entourage coming up the stairs. He hid behind a pillar and watched his brother and two other slaves pass. He recognized seven other merchants and their slaves. All these men wanted him dead. He pondered leaving, but his greed got the best of him. He hadn't been caught and was feeling invincible.

The young rabbi with the new following broke through the crowd. He had a look of determination on his face as he rushed up the steps. Andrew knew this magnetic man would create a distraction. He was about to follow him into the temple when he heard a commotion. The young Jewish leader was yelling and tipping over tables, driving everyone from the temple.

Angry merchants poured out of the front entrance. Tables and merchandise went toppling down the front steps. The Nazarene stood on the front steps and scooped up a pile of coins in his hands. He lifted them over his head and yelled, "You make a marketplace out of my Father's house!"

He threw the coins down the steps. He then walked down the steps. The crowd parted.

This was just the distraction Andrew had been waiting for. The thief dashed out onto the steps and began scooping up the coins.

Timothy saw his younger brother stuffing coins into his pockets.

He pointed at the steps and shouted, "Benjamin! My brother is the one you seek!"

Benjamin looked up and saw Andrew. The other merchants and landowners turned their attention to the top of the steps. A large crowd rushed up the stairs. Andrew tried to retreat but was surrounded.

Benjamin made his way through the crowd. He saw the quivering young man clutching silver coins to his chest. The other wealthy businessmen began chanting. "Kill him!"

Benjamin was surprised at the resemblance he had to his brother. He turned to Timothy. "You spoke the truth. You are released from bondage. Go back to Nain and take care of your mother and sisters."

The wealthy merchant handed Timothy a leather pouch filled with coins. Timothy and Andrew looked at one another. Timothy bowed to Benjamin, took the leather pouch and retreated down the steps.

Benjamin announced, "We will have an opportunity to accuse this swine in public. There will be a reckoning for his thievery!"

"The trial lasted less than fifteen minutes," Andrew said.

"You had a lot of people angry with you," said the Comforter.

Andrew felt sick. The futility of living a selfish existence had been laid out before him. "What a waste I have been," he mumbled. He slumped against the tree and closed the book in disgust.

"Nothing I create is a waste," said the Father. "There were many wasted opportunities. There was much wasted time. The total reliance on yourself for answers resulted in wasteful actions. These are truths about you. This does not mean *you* were a waste. I still remember the day the idea of you came to me. I was so excited to create all it means to be you. I had many plans for your life. I laid up many blessings for you."

"What do you mean, you laid up blessings for me?" Andrew asked.

The Father stood. Looking down, He spoke to the Comforter. "We will meet you at the eastern gate."

The Comforter nodded in agreement.

Andrew slowly rose, not knowing what was next.

The Father reached out and grabbed Andrew's hands. "Let me show you a glimpse of your blessings."

Andrew could feel the Father's words transport them. The tree on the hill vanished, and now they stood in the center of a massive granite building. Giant pillars went upward for miles. Large stone bins surrounded him on all sides. They were a hundred times taller than any building he had ever seen. At the bottom of each of them was a large wooden door. Rows of these containers stretched to infinity in all directions.

"Where are we?" Andrew's voice echoed through the overwhelming structure.

The Father smiled and raised his arms. "These are the storehouses of heaven. In each, I have stored up blessings for each of my children. Some choose paths that don't allow me to open their doors. Some of these storehouses won't be opened until they arrive home," the Father explained.

Andrew stood in awe. "Do I have one?"

The Father walked over to the storehouse in front of them. He crouched down and with both hands lifted the heavy wooden door. Golden grain began pouring out, surrounding Andrew's feet, then knees. The grain slowed as it met his waist. A tingling sensation crept through Andrew. He reached out and filled his hands with the amber granules. His spirit filled. A knowing set in, opening his mind. The plans and dreams that the Father had intended embraced him.

Andrew realized the potential he had squandered. He realized his choices had cut those gifts from his life.

"If I had only known, I would have lived a better life," Andrew whispered.

The Father shook his head. "Andrew, you could not even recognize the gifts that were right in front of you. I gave you loving parents. I gave you prosperity, health, creativity, and intelligence. I poured these things out to you from this very door."

Andrew sifted the flaxen kernels through his fingers. Flashes of consciousness flooded his mind.

The Father said, "There are many things in this storehouse I was not able to give. The good news is, your death was just the beginning of your life."

THIRTY-ONE

THE FATHER WAVED HIS HAND. All the grain was instantly pulled back into the storehouse. The booming sound of the slamming door echoed.

Andrew reached out and took the Father's hand. "Please forgive me. I was a selfish and fearful fool."

The Father kissed his forehead. He looked lovingly at Andrew. "My son has already forgiven you, Andrew. It is done. Let's go to the city. I have something I want to show you."

At the speed of thought, they were standing by the eastern gate of the city under a large arched entrance. Ornate gates met in the middle. Angels flew over and around the archway. The Comforter welcomed them back. But there seemed to be a tension filling the air around them, a calm before a storm.

The angel, Gabriel, stood watch above the gate. "When will He come?" he shouted.

The Father and Comforter smiled at one another. The Comforter looked up and replied, "I know, Gabe. I miss Him, too. He will return when the plan has been completed."

"Are you talking about the one who promised to see me in paradise?" Andrew asked.

They both laughed and hugged Andrew.

"Yes. He is coming home!"

Gabriel blew his trumpet and the ancient gate slowly swung open. Andrew looked up in awe as he passed under the giant archway. Millions were gathered for the coming celebration. Once inside, the Father held up Andrew's hand.

"This is Andrew. He heard my Son and believed."

The crowd roared and music and dancing commenced. Jacob broke through the crowd and ran to his son. They held each other close, and the crowd cheered the reunion.

"I am sorry for insisting on going down that hill on our donkeys. My stubbornness left you and the rest of the family without a father and husband," Jacob said.

"I am sorry for not becoming the son you raised," Andrew said to his father.

Jacob smiled and stroked his boy's hair. "I was a fool. I put too much emphasis on tradition. I never thought about what would be good for you. Please forgive me, Andrew."

They walked with the Father and the Comforter through the city. Shouts of welcome rang from the tops of roofs and open windows. They turned a corner and stopped in front of a sprawling park.

Andrew stared in awe at the scene in front of him. At the center of the park was a massive oak tree that climbed hundreds of miles into the sky. The enormous roots and trunk took up most of the verdant ground.

The Father gestured upward and said, "This is the tree of life. From this very tree came a seedling that was planted in the Garden of Eden. From these roots came a tree that grew outside of Jerusalem that was eventually hewn into a cross. When a new soul is born, a seedling is planted. It is a conduit to me. Whenever my children need to talk to me, I meet them under their tree. The same will happen for you, my son."

The crowd followed them as the Father walked toward a row of buildings lining the left side of the park. The crowd stopped when the Father walked up to a storefront.

The Comforter took Andrew and Jacob by the hand and led them to the front door. Andrew looked at the building. A large doorway and windows filled the entire front.

The Father gestured, and the front door opened. Jacob and Andrew walked inside the large store filled with merchandise. Rows and rows of items were neatly stacked on polished wooden shelves. There was a section with food items and additional shelves with jewelry, clothes, artwork, and even money.

"This is a beautiful store," Andrew said.

"Do you recognize any of these items?" the Comforter asked.

Andrew looked around again, and then shook his head 'no'.

The Father began to explain. He placed his arm around Andrew's shoulder. "These are all the items you stole in your lifetime."

Andrew was astonished. He had resold most of the items so fast that he hadn't paid any attention to what it was he had taken.

"What are they doing here?" Andrew asked.

"Your job is to catalog all these items. As people arrive, you will find their item and return it to them," the Comforter explained.

"I don't understand. They are no longer in need of any of these things. Why would they want them back?" he asked.

"This is not about them. It is about what you need. I have entrusted these items to you. You will make sure they are all returned," He instructed.

"Yes, sir," Andrew said.

The Father and Spirit hugged Andrew tightly, and he felt their unconditional love surge through him.

"If you have any questions, just ask. I will always hear you," the Father said.

Jacob and Andrew watched them walk out the front door of the store to the middle of the golden boulevard. Bright light enveloped them.

Andrew pressed his face against the glass of the store window. The crowd had moved back, leaving the men alone on the golden cobblestones. The two beings melted into one pillar of light. In the middle of the light, Andrew saw a shadow of the Father.

As the light subsided, Andrew and Jacob watched the Father strolling toward the holy temple. They followed the crowd. At the foot of the steps, silence fell over the crowd. Everyone seemed to sense that this was an intimate moment. A moment only they could share.

The Father ascended the thousand steps alone. He turned and raised his hands to the sky. He held that pose for a moment, and then turned and walked into the temple. Bells began to ring all over the city and the ground began to rumble beneath their feet.

Gabriel's trumpet sounded from the eastern gate.

Someone yelled and pointed toward the sky. "He is here!"

A golden streak of light roared over Gabriel's perch, heading toward the temple. An enormous cascade of sound, light, and love exploded out of the temple. A mighty wind rushed through the streets as the ground continued to shake. The pinks and oranges of sunrise silhouetted the temple.

Billions of people cheered as the Holy family were reunited. A triumphant brass chorus joined the angelic choir in celebration. Andrew stood there, dumbstruck by the majesty and power he was witnessing. Jacob held his son, as the entire city ignited with glee.

"He has invited us to the reunion banquet," Jacob yelled over the crowd.

"Why would we get to go?" Andrew asked.

Jacob laughed. "Everyone is invited."

Andrew laughed. "That must have been a huge tent you made, Father!"

The two chuckled and continued walking toward the brilliant

light. The warm pinks and oranges glistened off the golden streets. People were dancing and celebrating all around them.

Andrew asked his father, "What do you do when you want to talk to Him?"

Jacob was about to answer, but Andrew found himself suddenly alone in front of the large oak tree at the top of the hill. The city below was ablaze in light.

Andrew knelt in front of the tree. His tattered book lay propped up against the sturdy trunk.

"Are you coming?" said a large group bustling toward the city.

"I'll be right there," Andrew said, with a smile.

The group continued without him down the hill.

Andrew opened his book. There was a hand-written note on the front page.

"I planted this tree at the moment I thought of creating you. I knew one day you would return. Thank you for recognizing love when it came to you. You will be with me in paradise."

Andrew closed the book. He ran his hand across the bark of his tree. He knew this was the place he could come to be with Him. He turned and joined many others as they all ran boldly toward the throne of grace.

The End ... Is Just the Beginning ...

ACKNOWLEDGMENTS

Special thanks to Lori Lyn, Diana Ballew, Vickie Huddelston, and my wife Kimberly for their belief in this book.

ABOUT THE AUTHOR

Philip Bauer started his professional career in sales and marketing. His creative passions for song writing, art, and live performance were always in the background. During the nineties, his song writing became a reality when his first album got widespread airplay all across Europe. His artistic abilities came to the forefront when USA TODAY and The Kansas City Star placed several of his political cartoons on their editorial pages. He later had a weekly editorial cartoon called "Up Your News" in the City Sentinel in Oklahoma City.

Bauer hosted a weekly radio show called "Pathways to Recovery" where he interviewed guests about alcoholism and drug addiction. His own recovery has given him many opportunities to help others in their twelve-step journey. This on-air experience brought Philip many radio and television voice-over gigs.

In 2008, Philip decided he would use his ability to impersonate celebrities to his advantage. He studied the mannerisms and voice of Johnny Cash and performed a local show in Oklahoma City. The theater placed his performance on YouTube. Within weeks the venue was getting calls from producers all across the country. Within a month, Bauer quit his sales and marketing career and began touring his tribute to Johnny Cash. This show has now taken him all across the U.S., Mexico, Canada, Australia, and New Zealand. In 2015, his impersonation of the Man in Black gave him his own one hour nationally televised show on AXS TV's World's Greatest Tribute Bands live from Hollywood, California.

His writing career began with a dream about the afterlife and an oak tree. The image was so vivid to him that he began writing this, his first book.

Philip is married to the love of his life Kimberly. The couple resides in Oklahoma City, Oklahoma.

For more information:

97973420R00120

Made in the USA
Lexington, KY
02 September 2018